Guardian in the Wilderness

by Randy McCowan

ISBN 978-1-5323-3729-1

Editor: Paul Hoylen

Cover Art: Paul Hoylen
Book Design: Sherri McClellan

Olmesquite Publishing
Deming NM 88030

GRANDMAS

Dedicated to all the grandmas that help their families when called upon. To all the grandmas that are involved with their families, babysitting, or giving advice on everyday situations.

How many times have Mom and Dad said, "Go ask Grandma"? Parents may not have the answers to their children's questions, but Grandma does.

A grandmother's years of living has left her with knowledge, wisdom, and patience. She can answer the most difficult question in a way that a child can understand.

A grandmother can start a child laughing, and with her special hug, a grandmother can stop a child's crying. A grandmother's own children, when adults, still ask her for advice.
She will always be a mother and a grandmother. Often, just her love is all one needs.

ACKNOWLEDGEMENT

I would like to give credit to the people that have been involved in the writing and production of this book.

I am grateful to the proof readers, Princess Thompson, John Nash, Dr. G.W. Hartley, Doris Console and especially the typist my patient wife, Sally.

When you write a book that's all you think about. When you're awake and when you're sleeping. You are in your own world. I want to thank my editor, Paul Hoylen, and Bette Waters, the last person involved between the writing and the publishing process. I value her comments and suggestions. Also, Paul Hoylen's cartoon art work for the cover is unique in its perfection.

TABLE OF CONTENTS

PROLOGUE

Survival in the wilderness is more mental than physical. Survival means overcoming your challenges and co-existing with Mother Nature.

The greatest challenge is overcoming and conquering the fear that lies within oneself.

MATTHEW

Matthew and others like him were standing around the fiery fifty-five-gallon barrel.

It's another cold and windy night. They burned anything they could to keep warm.

An alley in the slums of Los Angeles was home to him for the past two months. Pan handling, rummaging through dumpsters, and working odd jobs to survive was the only life he knew in the streets.

Always alone during the day, his cohorts dubbed him "Loner." At night though, he could be found with others. This was just for protection; anyone alone at night could be beaten, robbed, or even killed.

Matthew pulled his dirty, frayed collar tight around his neck to keep warm. He buttoned the only two buttons on his worn, dirty, ragged coat. It wasn't much, but it was all he had. After another hour of keeping warm and listening to the others, Matthew decided to call it a night. He didn't say a lot even when others spoke to him. Matthew turned and walked away from the barrel to where he slept. The farther from the warmth of the burning barrel he went, the colder and darker the night became.

Matthew stayed in a cardboard box that was his shelter and

bed. He and another man wanted the cardboard box that had been vacated two days earlier. The box had belonged to a man named Jake before he left to walk the streets. He never came back. Matthew had to fight the other man for the box. Now it belonged to him. That's the law of the streets: You have to fight for what you want, and then fight to keep it.

He crawled into his box and closed the cardboard flaps to help keep out the cold. His bedding was nothing but dirty rags to lie on and cover with. Still, it was better than lying on the hard cold asphalt. Matthew tried to sleep. The same childhood memories came back again. In his adult years it didn't reoccur as often as when he was young. Even twenty-three years later, it still came around. It was almost like a shadow following him all the time. He never overcame the traumatic experience of what his mother did to him.

He was only five years old when she left him at the orphanage. She promised to return for him in two weeks. He waited and looked for her, but she never returned.

There wasn't a night that went by that he didn't cry himself to sleep. The more he wanted his mother, the more confused he became: "What did I do wrong? Why doesn't she come for me? Why did my mother stop loving me? Why would my mother do this to me?" he wondered.

The people at the orphanage were nice, but they could never take the place of his mother. They would hold him until he cried himself to sleep. He wished it was his mother holding him and telling him she loved him. The weeks and months turned into a year. By now his love for her had turned to anger and then to hate. As more years went by he hated her so much for what she did to him that he could never forgive her. As far as he was concerned, she was dead.

At a young age, he realized that the only one he could depend on was himself. He built an invisible wall around himself for protection. No one could get close to him and vice versa. No one would ever hurt him again.

He was in and out of five foster homes by the age of fourteen, never really fitting in at any of them. There was never a permanent place that he called home. Every time there was a problem, he was blamed for it: a fight at school, trouble with his foster siblings, or not getting along with his foster parents, Matthew would be sent back to the orphanage. He even ran away from the orphanage, but was found and returned. Matthew was labeled a trouble maker.

At the age of fourteen he was sent to yet another foster home. This one wasn't so bad.

He and his foster parents got along okay. Matthew stayed with them until he graduated from high school. When he turned eighteen he enlisted in the Army. He was sent to Afghanistan for one tour. He returned and finished his enlistment state-side. As far as Matthew was concerned, the Army was just another foster home, only bigger. Discharged on the East Coast, he hitched his way to the West Coast, still looking for a place to belong.

Matthew pulled his coat tighter and covered himself with a few more rags. It was getting colder.

It had been two years since his discharge from the Army. "There must be something more for me in life than this. There must be something I like to do," he thought out loud.

Matthew remembered one foster family did a lot of camping.

13

They hiked, fished, and did a lot of other things as a family. Matthew remembered he always had a good time. He also remembered enjoying it most when he was by himself. He liked how it felt hiking alone, feeling the freedom that surrounded him. At these times he thought that maybe he could live by himself in the mountains.

Matthew enjoyed the mountains because of the sense of adventure it gave him. He liked wondering what was on top or on the other side of the mountain, or where a game trail went. He liked to discover what was behind an outcropping of rocks.

Could he live in the wilderness?

Could he survive?

The more he thought about it, the more he came to the conclusion that maybe, just maybe, the mountains were where he belonged. At least now he had an idea in mind, a sense of direction and purpose.

Matthew decided to leave Los Angeles in the early morning and hitch-hike to Arizona or New Mexico, working along the way to support himself. Wherever he ended up, he would look for someone to teach him how to survive in the wilderness.

The next morning Matthew put everything he owned in two plastic bags. When asked by the others where he was going, he replied, "Just moving on."

Matthew took a last look at his surroundings and the men around him. "The young men are going nowhere and the old men have nowhere to go. That's not going to be me," he decided.

THE POST

Off Highway 180 in New Mexico near the Arizona/New Mexico state line is a dirt side road. In the mid-1800s it was one of the main roads heading west. On the road is an old building called the Post. A small room in the back of the old trading post is where Bill Collins calls home.

He woke routinely at 6:00 a.m. Slowly, he swung his legs around and off his single bed. When his feet touched the floor, he slowly stood. After stretching with stiffness, he got dressed and walked over to the sink. He brushed his teeth, then splashed cold water on his face. "Ready to meet the day," he said out loud. Before he walked away he looked in the mirror. His once coal-black hair was white as the snow that had been falling all night. His face showed the traces that only time can leave. At the age of eighty-four and now alone, Bill spent a lot of time remembering the past. Now days his memories are his only companions.

He walked out of his living quarters into the store. He stopped and placed another piece of pine on the carpet of red-orange coals in the wood-burning stove. A couple of logs at night kept the place toasty until morning; a few more in the morning would keep it warm the rest of the day.

Bill put on a pot of coffee, and then started cooking his

breakfast on a small stove behind the counter. One egg and a piece of toast is all he eats. A cup of coffee during breakfast, and another after, tops everything. Before his second cup he looked up at the clock. "Seven o'clock, time to open," he said.

He walked to the front of the store. At the window he turned over the Open/Closed sign. Unlocking the door, he looked out the window. The snow had stopped falling. Winter was not his favorite time of year, but there was nothing he could do about that.

Before he stepped away from the door, he reached up and tapped the little bell mounted above the door. It made a lively ringing sound. The bell lets him know when a customer enters. "I love that sound," he said and smiled. Once back in his chair, he poured his coffee.

"I wonder if anything exciting will happen today," he asked himself. Before he could take a sip of his coffee, he heard scratching at the back door, "Uh-oh, I forgot to let the cat in." He slowly got up from his chair, walked over and opened the back door. But before he could open it all the way, Midnight squeezed her way in. At night she slept in the wood shed. During the day, she prowled around the store. Eventually she would curl up in front of the wood-burning stove.

Bill sat back down in his chair, looked at Midnight and asked, "Can I drink my coffee now, Midnight?" Bill was half expecting the cat to answer.

While drinking his morning coffee, his thoughts routinely returned to years gone by. He remembered his wife and children. The memories of raising his family will last forever—as will all the enjoyable times his family spent together, especially the holidays.

His wife's love made everything possible. She was both his and the children's guiding light. They raised four children in Santa Fe, New Mexico. All four were married now and had their own families. Three moved out of state and one still lives in Santa Fe. After the kids were gone, Bill and his wife stayed in Santa Fe until her death three years ago. Bill sold the house and decided to move back to the old trading post.

Bill and his two sisters were born in the family house that once stood behind the Post. They grew up in the trading post and knew all about the business. Coming back to the Post gave Bill something to do.

Highway 180 was about two miles from the Post. It by-passed the dirt road to the Post. Bill knew business would be slow, but this really didn't matter; he had his gas company pension plus Social Security. His business was seasonal. Customers were hunters and people from the campgrounds located nearby. Also, the more Bill thought about it, the more he realized that he is carrying on the family tradition.

Bill's great-grandfather built the trading Post in 1869. At eighteen his great-grandfather was a Confederate soldier in the Civil War. After the war he went back home to Arkansas. Everything there had been destroyed. The house was burned and his folks killed. With nothing left, he headed west to start a new life. He got a job working on one of the wagon trains bound for California.

When the wagon train passed through New Mexico Territory, he left the train to strike out on his own. For the next two years he survived by trapping and trading his goods to wagon trains heading west. Every once in a while the people passing through would tell of problems with the Apaches elsewhere. He knew about the Apaches, but had no problems with them thus far; he had even traded with some of them. Trading and selling his goods was so steady that he decided to build a trading post. Within a couple of months the trading post was built and open. It was the only place to buy or trade supplies for miles in any direction. More than once, customers would ask, "What do you call this place?"

"It's just a trading post" he would answer. "Never gave it a name."

It wasn't too long before customers started calling it the Post. Even his great-grandfather liked that name. The Post kept him really busy and before he knew it, a year had gone by.

During that year Apache raiding was on the rise. Stories were told by people passing through. The army patrolled the roads and mountains, keeping the Apaches in check. The patrols would stop by and keep him informed of any Apache trouble. Great-grandfather felt sympathy for the Apaches. He knew first-hand how it felt to have your land destroyed and your family killed.

He had seen enough fighting and killing in the war. On the other hand, he would do what he had to do to protect his own.

Busy days and quiet nights were his day and night routine. The quiet nights gave him the feeling of loneliness. Finally, he came to the decision that he had been struggling with for the past five or six months; he needed a companion; more than a companion, he needed a wife.

Even with the stories of Apache raids going on, some of the peaceful Apache women and a few Apache men had been trading with him. They had become quite friendly. He had learned enough of their language to communicate with them.

One day when they came to trade, he noticed that there was an Indian woman with them that wasn't Apache. In talking to them, he found out that she was Navajo. She had been captured in a raid about a month ago. She was a slave of the Apache women. Her job was cooking and doing other chores in camp. Great-grandfather told them he wanted to trade something for her. When the women finished their trading, they took her and left. Two weeks later, they came in and traded her for two blankets and glass beads. It was a good trade. They stayed together for forty-three years. Within the first four years, they built a house and were blessed with two sons.

But renegade Apaches that did not want peace with the white man were raiding and burning settlements and killing settlers. The Apaches wanted the white man out of their territory—it was their land.

Early one morning, a large group of Apaches attacked and burned the Post to the ground. The most tragic loss was the death of their youngest son.

He was outside doing his morning chores. When the raid occurred, he was shot down between the barn and the house.

The rest of the family survived because they were in the house and ready to fight. But what really saved them were the two squads of soldiers that arrived in time to run off the raiding Apaches. They gave chase, but never caught the renegades. Great-grandfather never did find out which groups of Apaches were responsible for their son's death.

They weren't quitters and weren't going to be discouraged by renegade Apaches or anyone else.

They buried their son out behind their house and rebuilt the Post. They were never bothered by Apaches again.

The Post has been passed down from generation to generation. Bill's father and mother were the last ones to keep the Post open. After they both died, the Post was closed.

Three years after the closing, a forest fire raged though the mountains, burning down the old family house. Luckily, the trading post was spared.

Bill brought his thoughts to the present. It looked like just about everything and everyone centered around the Post was gone. He started laughing, then talking out loud. "Life has some strange and surprising twists and turns. You never know where life's path will lead you. Here I am, ending up where I started out eighty-four years ago. What will happen to the Post when I'm gone?" he asked himself.

BILL MEETS MATTHEW

Without customers all morning, the time passed slowly. Eventually it was lunch time. "After I eat, I'll take my afternoon nap," Bill said to himself. When he finished eating, he sat in his favorite chair and closed his eyes. He had just started to doze off when the bell at the door jingled. "There goes my afternoon nap." Bill looked towards the front of the store. A young man who appeared to be in his mid-20s, had just entered.

"Stomp the snow off your feet and come on in!" yelled Bill.

He wore his hat low, partially covering his face, shoulder length hair, and a stubble beard. He looked like an outdoorsman. He took off his pack, and set it on the floor near the door. Strapped on top of the pack was his bedroll and blanket. The young man began browsing around. "Let me know if I can help you with anything," said Bill. Without answering, the young man kept walking around and looking up one aisle, then down another. Bill was standing behind the counter closely watching the young man. "He's a little suspicious," Bill thought to himself. Bill wasn't taking any chances. He lowered his hand out of sight below the counter top and placed it around the grip of his loaded .45 pistol. "I've never been robbed and I am not going to be robbed now," he thought to himself. Bill's eyes and attention were still on the young man.

Finally, after wandering around and looking, the young man approached the counter.

"Is there anyone around here that can teach me how to survive in the wild?" he asked.

"You mean some of the primitive sites where you could rough it for a couple of weeks?"

"No, I don't mean that."

"I don't understand. You come in here with a pack and bedroll. Its looks to me like you've already been camping in the mountains."

"True, but that isn't what I'm talking about. How many people that hike a lot and camp out could actually survive in the wild if they had to? Now days you buy everything from water to anything else you need. Some of the supplies have been modernized with technology. There is dehydrated food, battery-operated gloves for warmth, just to name a few. Buy what you need. That's all you have to do. Everything's at your finger tips. I want to go way back in the mountains and wilderness. I want to go where most people don't go. I want to survive off the land."

Bill thought to himself: "It sounds like he wants to disappear. Is he running away from something? Maybe he's wanted by the police. I know the sheriff in this area. He would have notified me if anyone was wanted. Why am I thinking these things? After all, it's none of my business. Maybe he just wants to live in the mountains."

Again, the young man asked, "Is there anyone around here who can teach me how to survive in the wild?"

"Not around here."

The young man stuck out his right hand. "My name is Matthew Russ, What's yours?"
Still keeping his left hand on his pistol, Bill shook hands. "Bill Collins is my name."

"I like your collection of old Army and Apache pictures. Your display of old weapons used by the Army and the Apaches is very interesting. You have your own little museum."
"A lot of old stuff," replied Bill. Feeling no threat, Bill now took his hand off his pistol.

"It looks to me like you need an Indian or a mountain man to show you the traditional ways. Your chance of finding one here is probably next to none. If you did find an Indian he probably wouldn't teach you because you're not Indian. You're not, are you?" asked Bill.

"I don't know, but I doubt it."

"You know, the more I think about it, somewhere in the mountains there probably is someone who could teach you, but I don't know who."

"What do you mean, someone 'but you don't know who?'" asked Matthew.

"About two years ago, I was letting in my cat, Midnight. When I opened the back door I was surprised to see a cardboard box on the step. In the box were a lot of hand-made items. There were arrowheads, pottery, knives, arrows and a lot of turquoise jewelry. Also, there was a note. Whoever the person was, they wanted to trade for salt, flour, coffee and other supplies. I thought it was a fair trade. I filled the box and placed it outside that night. The next morning it was gone. This trade has been going on ever since."

"How often do these trades happen?"

"Maybe two or three times a year. For some reason, the trade stops in the early winter."

"You never ever caught a glimpse of the person?"

"Never tried, I might ruin a good trade," chuckled Bill.

"Where would I begin to look for this person?" asked Matthew.

"That's a good question. There are a lot of mountains and wilderness areas out there. In Arizona you have the White Mountains, Chiricahua Mountains, and the Pedregosa Mountains close to the state line. In Arizona and New Mexico there's the Peloncillo Mountains. Up here where we are, is the Gila Wilderness, the Mogollon Mountains, Black Range, Tularosa Mountains, and the San Mateo Mountains. I'm just naming the largest mountain ranges. There are still a lot of smaller ranges. It won't be easy finding who you're looking for.

"If I were you, I'd follow the hiking trails out of the lower mountains and head south towards the border. It's a little warmer south. In the lower mountains the snow has stopped and started melting by now. We still have snow up here. But it's just about finished for the year. Further up north, it's still cold and snowing; about another month before it's through. Remember, I told you the trade stops in the first part of winter. That's why I think whoever it is, goes south where it's warmer. Maybe even as far as Mexico. I don't know."

"I'll give it a try." Matthew filled his pack buying everything he needed to last two or three weeks.

"Stay on the hiking trails. There are other hikers that you'll probably meet up with. Also, there are campsites all along the trails. How are you going to know the person when you find him or her?"

"I don't know, but I'm sure I'll know when the time comes."

As Matthew left the store, Bill yelled, "Good luck!" As the door closed, Bill thought to himself, "I think I like that young fella."

Early the next morning, Matthew headed into the mountains, finding the trail Bill told him about that headed southwest. He hiked all morning before finally stopping to eat lunch. As soon as he ate, he was off again. Two, then three more hours passed. During this time he had come across three other hikers. He knew none of them were who he was looking for. Then he asked himself. "How will I know when I find the one I'm looking for?"

It was getting dark when he stopped at one of the campsites along the trail. "I'll start again in the morning." Matthew began to make camp for the night. As he started the fire with an automatic igniter, he asked himself, "How would I start a fire without the igniter or matches? What if I didn't have cans and packets of dehydrated food? What if I didn't have this solar blanket to keep warm? How about no flashlight? If I wasn't close to water, and had no bottled water, what would I do? If I didn't have all these conveniences, I could die out here. The one item that could save someone would be a cell phone, but I've been told the phone doesn't always work in the mountains." Matthew, now more than ever, was determined to find whoever it is that could teach him what he needed to know.

Morning after morning, day after day, he hiked and hiked. The lower he hiked out of the mountains, the more people he met on the trails and in the campsites. He had the feeling, for some reason, that the person he was looking for would not be found here but higher up in the mountains. It had been a week and a half since he left the Post; Matthew was running low on supplies. He headed back to the Post.

Along the trail were signs showing all the different hiking trails. One of the signs showed a different trail going back; it was a lower trail but connected to the higher trail that he came in on. After he saw the sign, he remembered seeing where the two trails met. The return trail ended up just as long and disappointing as the trail he went out on. Finally, he arrived at the Post.

Bill was stocking and rearranging one of the shelves when the bell at the door jingled. Bill looked toward the door. When he saw it was Matthew, he said, "You're back. Did you find who you were looking for?"

"No."

"There's a lot of mountains and wilderness out there. And you're only looking for one person. You'll just have to keep looking. But you must be doing something right; you found your way back. Believe it or not, some people can even get lost on the trail," Bill said smiling.

"I had better find what I'm looking for this time out. After I buy supplies, I'll be out of money," said Matthew. He again filled his pack with everything he needed. Matthew told Bill he would head out early in the morning. Bill told him to head east where he'd find the main trail. When he left, Bill once again wished him good luck.

Matthew spent another three weeks in the mountains. It was no different than the first time out—just more hikers and more campsites. Once again he came up empty-handed. Disappointed and disgusted, he headed back to the Post. When he returned, Bill was glad to see him. Before Bill could say anything, Matthew said, "It's the same as last time—nothing. Like you said, there are plenty of mountains and wilderness out there. I could spend the rest of my life looking. We don't know if he or she is even out there. Maybe whoever it is isn't around here anymore."

Bill smiled and said, "Whoever is out there is still there."

"What makes you so certain?"

Bill pointed to the box on the floor. "It was on the doorstep two mornings ago, filled with trade items, like always."

"This is encouraging. "Now, I'm more determined to find who's out there."

"If I remember right, the last time you bought supplies you spent the last of your money!"

"Yeah, I plan on selling some of my gear and anything else I can sell. Maybe I'll even work somewhere and save up enough money to head out again."

"I have a better idea. I could use some help around the Post. Give me a couple weeks work and I'll trade you supplies. After all, you might as well start trading now. If you end up living in the mountains, there's no place to spend your money out there." Matthew laughed and said, "It's a trade, Bill." Then they shook hands.

"Two weeks from now the heavy snow up high will be pretty much gone. The rivers will be running full. The trail will lead you high into the mountains. Beyond the trail is nothing but rough, rocky wilderness. It's full of nothing but arroyos and thick, scattered forest, almost impossible to access. Up high, there's nothing but rock. No one goes up there. It's unlivable unless you're a mountain goat. Just be careful if you decide to go off the trail. You could climb up high, if possible, to find an observation point, but you would only see miles and miles of wilderness. Maybe leaving the trail is a bad idea," said Bill. "You have your sleeping bag, why don't you just sleep in the back room until you leave?"

"Good idea."

Two weeks later Matthew was ready to go. Bill gave him supplies for the two weeks work. "Good luck!" Bill said as Matthew headed into the mountains for the third time. But this time they both knew the person he was looking for was still out there.

ANOTHER SEARCH

Matthew had been searching for over two weeks. He got caught in a rain storm late one afternoon.

He managed to find shelter in an old mine; abandoned mines could be found throughout the mountains. He spent the night, then left early the next morning.

He met a few hikers at the lower elevations, but knew they weren't who he was searching for. He left the trail and climbed to the top of one of the higher mountains. From there he could see for miles, but like Bill had told him, he could see only wilderness. It seemed to go forever in every direction.

Matthew began to descend the other side of the mountain. It didn't take him long to realize that it was just as hard going down as coming up. It was slippery because of the storm the night before.

About half-way down he came across a game trail and decided to follow it; following the game trail made his hiking a little easier. It led him to a small stream that he hoped would eventually flow into one of the rivers below. He followed it the rest of the day, then made camp for the night.

The next day he continued following it. Matthew finally reached the river; it was high and moving fast. The storm two nights before had brought a lot of rain to the mountains. With just a few hours of daylight left, Matthew found shelter. The next morning he headed down-river, hiking the banks of the swollen river until late afternoon. All along the river bank were piles of brush and branches.

There were small animals that had been flushed out of their underground burrows and had drowned. Their carcasses were laying on the river edge. Matthew saw what appeared to be an animal carcass partly submerged in a shallow pool of water. When Matthew got closer to take a better look, he was taken back by surprise. It was a human body — a woman's body in among the debris. Her long black hair was muddy, matted and tangled; her clothes were muddy and torn.

"How did a woman end up out here in the middle of nowhere?" he asked himself. "The least I can do is pull her out of the water and bury her."

He grabbed her head of hair and started to pull the body onto the bank. The body moved slightly. Matthew let go and jumped back. "She isn't dead!" he said out loud. He finished pulling her onto the bank. When he turned her over, he was shocked. It was a man, an Indian. He looked like some of the Indians in the pictures at Bill's trading post. All Matthew could think of was that he had pulled the past up from a watery grave.

Matthew performed CPR and the man started coughing and spitting up water. He looked up at Matthew, and then closed his eyes.

He knew the man was hurt, cold, and exhausted. Matthew covered him with a blanket, and then built a fire. "I'll take him down below tomorrow if he can travel," Matthew thought to himself. He made himself comfortable and fell asleep. He woke up several times in the night, checked on the man, and added more wood to the fire.

The injured Indian was the first to awake. He looked around trying to figure out what had happened. "How did I get here? I remembered the swift current pulling me under, but that is all."

The Indian looked over at the man sleeping. "He must have saved my life. I wonder who he is, and what's he doing up here. Hikers don't come this high. There are no hiking trails.

"He might be one of them. Maybe he plans on taking me back. I will have to be careful with my answers for whatever questions he might ask. I'll watch him closely until I find out who he is and what he's doing here," the Indian thought to himself.

Matthew awoke and walked over to the man.

"What happened? I found you unconscious, almost drowned and hanging on to a tree branch."

"I tried to cross the swollen river. I slipped and went under. I remember being carried away by the strong current. That's all I remember."

"You're lucky I found you. My name is Matthew."

"Thanks for saving my life. My name is Manuel."

"You're bruised and cut up. I know you must hurt all over. Rest as long as you want. When you feel up to it, we'll go down below and have you taken care of," Matthew said.

"I'll be okay," replied Manuel. "I probably look worse than I feel. We have to move to a safer place."

"What do you mean a 'safer place'?" asked Matthew.

Manuel didn't answer. Instead, he slowly got up and began painfully heading up the mountain. "Follow me," he said. Matthew followed him wondering where they were going. There was no trail. Manuel moved slowly because of his injuries. After about forty-five minutes, they stopped for a break.

"Why are we going this high in the mountains?" asked Matthew. "I can get you help down below."

Once again, Manuel didn't answer. "Let's go," he said. Matthew followed.

"There's something mysterious about this Indian -looking man," Matthew thought to himself.

Wherever they were headed, he knew they were going deeper and higher into the wilderness. It was hard to believe that anyone could live out here. They stopped again.

Matthew tried to start a conversation. Manuel only seemed interested in looking back at the direction they had just come from. It was almost like he was worried about someone following them.

Finally they were on a game trail. They started climbing off the trail, straight up the mountain. Near the top, they stopped among the rocks.

"Why are we stopping again so soon? But that's okay if you're tired," Matthew said. Manuel didn't answer. Instead, he grabbed the branch of a thick bush directly in front of him. Pulling it to him, he uncovered a small crevice in the rocks. The opening allowed enough light so that Matthew could see a crawl space.

Manuel led the way. They crawled no more than five or six feet before they were able to stand up. They were in the middle of a large cavern.

"Stay here," he told Matthew.

Manuel then went over to the rock wall and pulled out a hunting knife. Before Matthew had time to think about what was happening, Manuel was striking a rock against the knife blade over some small twigs. Before long he started a fire. He then put the knife down.

Silently, Matthew exhaled the breath he had been holding. He felt more relaxed. The fire provided light for the cavern. The smoke disappeared through the cracks in the rock overhead.

"Who is this man? Where am I?" Matthew wondered. He looked around the cavern. Over against the wall he saw a box of articles like the ones at the Post. There were also baskets full of cactus apples, mesquite beans, piñon nuts and other food items. Hanging from a yucca rack against the wall were strips of dried meat. He walked over to the wall to get a better look. There were bowls, bows and arrows, arrowheads, and turquoise jewelry.

Matthew said to himself, "It's him!" Before he could stop himself, he blurted out "You're the one!" He turned around.

"What do you mean, 'You're the one'? What are you doing up here?" asked Manuel.

"You're the one who leaves the box at Bill's trading post."

Manuel was hesitant. He paused before answering, "Yes, I am."

"I've been hiking these mountains for almost two months trying to find you."

"What for? Why is it so important for you to find me?"

"Living and surviving in the wilderness like the Indians and mountain men did, is what I want to do. I feel that I belong here in the mountains. But I don't know how to live in the wilderness. I need somebody to teach me. I think you're the one," answered Matthew.

"Is that the real reason you're here? Tell me the truth,"

"That's the truth; I have no reason to lie. What I've told you is the truth."

"Don't you have a family and a home somewhere?" asked Manuel.

"No."

"Sit down and tell me more about yourself."

When he had finished, Manuel shook his hand. "You saved my life. I can never do enough to repay you. Teaching you how to survive in the wild is the least I can do. Sorry about all the questions, but I can't take any chances."

"What do you mean, 'Can't take any chances'? What's the mystery of not being seen at the trading post? Why do you live up here? Why are you dressed like a mountain man and look like an Indian?"

"My father is Mexican and Mescalero Apache. My mother is Chiricahua Apache. Her grandmother was with Chief Victorio when he was killed in the Tres Castillos Mountains in Chihuahua, Mexico in 1880. She was only five years old.

"The women and children were taken captive and given or sold to Mexican families to be used as servants or to be traded. She and her mother were separated. She never saw her mother again. The Mexican family that raised her treated

34

her like family.

"Even so, being raised as a Mexican didn't really change her. She never forgot she was Apache, or forgot wanting to live free.

"At the age of eleven years old, she escaped into the mountains and found other Apaches. There she lived, married, and spent the rest of her life with her own people.

"The Apache way of life has been passed down through my family from generation to generation.

"I live up here alone and I'm suspicious of anyone this high in the mountains. I prospect in the old mines and have found a little gold. During the winter I trade the gold in Mexico. If I see anyone, I have to be careful. I could be followed. That's why I don't trade at the Post during the day. We'll stay here tonight.

"Maybe Matthew is telling the truth, maybe not." Manuel thought to himself. "I'll show him some basic things about survival. I want to make sure that's all he's after. When I feel he's telling the truth and I know I can trust him, I'll tell him the truth about myself."

The next morning, Matthew made the coffee for himself and Manuel. "Are you sure you don't want me to take you down below for medical attention?"

"I'm sure."

"Last night I told you I would teach you how to live in the wilderness. But there are a few things I can't teach you. One important thing you must never forget: In our society, man is the top of the food chain. We rely on animals for food, either domestic or wild. It's much different out here. In Mother

Nature's world, the food chain is reversed. Here, we have become part of nature's food chain.

"Bears, mountain lions, wolves, and snakes are some of the predators. Out here, we are the hunted. We are on the bottom of the food chain. We're like two ants in the wilderness.

"Some fruits and plants can also be poisonous. I'll show you what's safe to eat and what's not.

"Something else you must not forget: Out here you must know what to do, and what not to do. You will develop your senses on your own. That's something I can't teach you. Survival is more mental than physical. Watch and learn from the movement of the birds and animals. Their movement can alert you to danger, or near-by hunters and hikers.

"Much of the time you'll be by yourself. One mistake out here could cost you your life. Be careful. For now, we'll just camp and move through the mountains."

Three weeks had passed since Manuel's ordeal. He had fully recovered. During that time a strong friendship was developing between the two. For the first time in his life, Matthew knew how it was to have a close friend. Manuel was someone he could talk to about anything. They would sit around the campfire and talk for hours on end. From their talks, Manuel was convinced that Matthew was telling the truth. He never asked any more personal questions. He just asked about year-around weather in the mountains, species of animals, and dangers in the wilderness.

All he wanted was to learn to survive in the wild. If they were to stay together Manuel should tell him the truth.

One night while sitting around the campfire, Manuel decided

to tell Matthew about himself. Looking at him, with a serious look on his face, he said, "Trust and honesty are part of any relationship between two people. There is something I have to tell you about myself. Then you will understand why I'm out here.

"First of all, my name is not Manuel. My real name is Carlos Muñoz.

Secondly, I'm a fugitive."

"What?" Matthew said, with a shocked look on his face.

"Yes, I'm wanted in both Mexico and the United States."

"I was a captain of a special Mexican police task force in Agua Prieta, Mexico. Our job was to investigate and combat the drug cartels. There were ten officers that made up our special unit.

"There can be corruption even in an elite task force like ours. Myself and two of my closest officers, who I've known for a long time, were suspicious of three of our own men. We were involved in a lengthy investigation of them to obtain enough evidence to file charges. The rest of the force knew nothing of this. My task force and another unit joined together to raid a house belonging to a drug cartel. At night we surrounded the house. Our surprise raid was supposed to catch them off guard. Before I could give the signal to surround the house we were fired on. There was no way they knew we were coming unless they had been tipped off. The shooting from the house stopped. We hadn't even exchanged gun fire. It didn't make any sense at all.

"From the house someone, yelled, 'Captain Muñoz! This is not the deal you promised. Just like in the past, you've been paid off to leave us alone. For the last two years we've been working together. We pay you and you don't bother us. You make sure that we can get our drugs across the border. Why are you doing this? Haven't we paid you enough?'

"The men that were closest to me looked at me in disbelief. Then one of my men who was under investigation yelled, 'He's one of them!'

"That's not true, it's a lie!" I yelled back. Then I gave the order, and we fired at the house. They returned fire. Bullets were flying everywhere. I took cover. The bullets, rocks, and dirt were ricocheting all around me. I fired toward the house. I was taking fire from another direction. Then I realized what was happening. The three men under investigation were also trying to kill me. If I was killed during an operation it wouldn't arouse any suspicion.

"I fired back hitting one of them. One of the other two yelled, 'The captain shot one of his own men!'

"Another one of my men ran over to the one I had shot. He knelt down to see how bad he was. He rose up, looking at me. 'He's dead, captain!' he yelled.

"Before he could say or do anything else, more shooting came from the house. He took cover. We exchanged gun fire with the men inside the house until the situation was secured. After all the firing had stopped, my men went inside the house to make arrests.

"One of my trusted officers came up to me and said, 'You better get out of here while you can. With what the men heard and saw tonight I don't think they would believe you. I know the one you shot was trying to kill you, but they don't know.

We can't tell the rest of the men why, without revealing the investigation. What was yelled from the house didn't help you either. For now, let's get you out of here.'

"We left in his official car and headed for the border. We both agreed that the safest place for me would be across the border into the United States.

"If I stayed in Mexico, the drug cartel or my own men might have tried to kill me. We had both been across the border so many times that we had no problem crossing. He let me off on one of the side roads leading into the mountains."

"I guess you're going to live in the mountains," he said.

"I told him the mountains are my second home; no one would find me.

"Then he advised me not to return to Mexico, saying, 'When everyone finds out what happened, you will be looked upon as a fugitive. Both Mexico and the United States will be looking for you. I will keep investigating the other two officers. I know you have ways of crossing the border, but I would wait until this situation settles down. Be patient. I will tell your family what happened tonight. As a precaution, I will move them to a safe place. I will make sure they are well protected, Good luck.' Then he retuned to Mexico."

"You mentioned family," Matthew said.

"Yes, I am married and have two children — a boy and a girl. My grandmother also lives with us. She's ninety-two years old and in a wheel chair. Her body may be old, but her mind is young. Her wisdom, advice, and stories sometimes give answers to our every-day problems. Her stories have been passed down from generation to generation. All her stories contain a lesson in life. Family makes life worth living. There is nothing more important, Matthew. I really miss them." said Carlos.

Matthew could tell it was hard for Carlos to talk about his family, so he changed the subject.

"What do you do up here to help pass the time?" Matthew asked.

"I have camps throughout the wilderness. I spend my time hunting and gathering firewood. Supplying the camps takes up most of my time, even though I go to Mexico for most of the winter. When I return, a late snow might keep me snowed in. During monsoon season the rain might also keep me in isolation. During these times I keep busy making things or drying food for storage. Also, I have to stay in hiding. I stay out of sight when hiking between camps. There is always something to do. Time up here is endless."

MEXICO

"We need to go to Mexico," said Carlos.

"What for?" asked Matthew.

"Two things of importance: I want to tell my family that you saved my life, and I want to see my family. I will also teach you some things on the trip there and more when we return."

"I thought you were not to return to Mexico until you were proven innocent."

"I know. This isn't my first trip back. After I was in the mountains for three months I couldn't stand being away from my family. I don't worry about being caught. I take the trails my ancestors did when moving between the United States and Mexico, and I have plenty of hiding places.

"Also, I know my family will feel better knowing that I am not up here alone. We will use the same trail and some hiding places that my ancestors used. We will avoid anyone we see. You can go to the Post to trade during the day. If you meet other hikers, make sure you're not followed when you return; you might lead someone to our camp. If I am ever caught, you might also be in trouble. Guilt by association, you know. You're better off to avoid people, if possible," said Carlos.

"The less contact I have with people, the better I like it," Matthew replied.

Carlos let out a little laugh.

"What's so funny?" asked Matthew.

"Out here we're surrounded by all the freedom a man would ever want. But in a way we're prisoners of our own freedom. Take some of your supplies back to the Post," Carlos said. "Some things you won't need. We can trade them for useful items, especially coffee, I love my coffee."

The next day Matthew left for the trading post. It took him three days to come down out of the mountains and on to a lower trail, and another half-day before he reached the Post.

As he entered, he saw Bill behind the counter. "Did you find who you were looking for?" Bill asked.

"I sure did," answered Matthew. "And he agreed to teach me all the survival ways. He sent me back with some things that I wouldn't need."

"Who was it that you found?" asked Bill. Matthew hated to lie to Bill. If it weren't for Bill, Matthew could not have gone out that last time. Maybe some day he could tell him the truth.

"He's just some old mountain man that doesn't like civilization. He likes being alone," answered Matthew.

Matthew finished trading with Bill, but before he left he wandered into the museum section of the store. Pretending to look at the items for sale, he picked up an old clay pot. While looking at it he glanced over at the bulletin board. Surrounded by advertisement and "for-sale" flyers was a wanted poster. When he saw it, he about dropped the pot. It was Carlos all right. His hair was short, but it was Carlos. Matthew said good-bye, then headed back into the wilderness.

It was a windy morning when they left for Mexico. They carried everything they needed in deerskin bags.

"We have plenty of water in the mountains, but what happens when we reach the desert?" asked Matthew.

"Don't worry," Carlos said. "I've gathered discarded water bottles from hunters, hikers, campers, and illegals. The bottles are filled and buried throughout the desert along with other supplies."

After four days of hiking, they were in Arizona. It would take about two weeks to reach the border. After another three days of hiking, they were in the Peloncillo Mountains. Another five days and they were right above the San Simon Valley.

"How are we going to cross without being seen?" asked Matthew.

"Do you see that ranch house?" asked Carlos.

"Yeah," answered Matthew"

"My cousin is the ranch foreman. He always helps me. He will get us to the Chiricahua Mountains."

When they reached the ranch house, they went inside and met the cousin and his family. Carlos told them how Matthew had saved him. They ate dinner and spent the night.

Early the next morning they were ready to leave. When Matthew stepped outside he couldn't believe what he saw: there were four cowboys and a small herd of cattle ready to go.

"This is the way I always cross through open areas. Just cowboys herding cattle," said Carlos with a smile. By the end of the day they were at another ranch house near the base of the Chiricahua Mountains. Carlos and Matthew went into the mountains. The cowboys and the cattle headed out to the ranch.

After five more days of hiking and camping, the border fence came into view. It seemed to go forever in both directions.

"How are we going to get over the fence once we get there?"

asked Matthew.

"We're not. That is a solid rock cliff in front of us, over two hundred feet high and five to six hundred yards in length. The fence stopped at each end. It was natural stone wall impossible to climb. Down at its base were large boulders, cactus, and thick mesquite. Hidden in the rocks and mesquite is a secret tunnel. This tunnel was known only to the Apaches. The Apaches that scouted for the U.S. Army knew of the tunnel, but they dared not tell. To reveal this secret tunnel meant death. My great grandmother and her people used this tunnel when being pursued by the U.S. or the Mexican Army. Both entrances are concealed on either side of the border," said Carlos.

Carlos pointed to the lone house directly in front of them. "We will spend the night there."

"Is the old house vacant?"

Before Carlos could answer, Matthews's heart started pounding.

"Look, Carlos!"

A Border Patrol agent was coming out of the house. All Matthew could think of was that they were caught! He looked at Carlos, not knowing what they are going to do. Was Carlos going to run, fight, or just give up? The agent was armed. Maybe they had no choice but to give up. Now the agent was almost directly in front of them. Whatever Carlos was going to do, Matthew was with him. He was ready. To Matthew's surprise, the agent asked Carlos who his friend was.

"That's Matthew," said Carlos. The agent shook Matthew's hand.

"My name's Hector. A friend of my cousin is a friend of mine," he said. "Let's go into the house." As they walked to the house, Matthew was shaking his head and softly muttering to himself, "I don't believe this." Once in the house, he met Hectors' wife and three kids. Once again Carlos told the story about Matthew.

Hector explained to Matthew that some of the agents on both sides of the border know that Carlos is innocent. They help him whenever he wants to cross the border.

"By the way, Carlos, your family has been notified that you're coming," said the cousin. "Someone will be waiting for you on the other side."

Carlos and Matthew ate, then rested. Just before dark they left the house accompanied by the cousin in uniform. If by chance they were seen with an agent, no one would think anything of it.

They made their way to the high inaccessible cliff. After they zigzagged among the cactus, mesquite, and rocks, they stopped in front of a large prickly pear cactus.

Carlos and his cousin moved some of the rocks aside that were in front of the cactus so they could begin digging in the sand.

"Here it is," said Carlos. When the cousin pushed some sand away, Matthew could see the trap door. The cousin pulled the door open. Carlos held the door open while his cousin reached down and brought up an old lantern, then lit it.

When the lantern was lit, Matthew could see a wooden ladder going down to the tunnel below. Carlos and Matthew climbed down into the tunnel. The cousin passed down the lantern and their gear. "I'll let the other end know you're on your way." He said good-bye, and closed the door. From below, they could hear him covering it back over.

Carlos and Matthew walked for about forty-five minutes before reaching the end of the tunnel. Carlos climbed up a wooden ladder and gave a whistle.

A whistle from the outside echoed back. The door was opened by someone outside. When they climbed out of the tunnel they were greeted by two men. Matthew calmly looked at them.

"I'm not even going to act surprised when he tells me they're his cousins," he thought to himself.

The men hugged and shook hands with Carlos.

"Meet my brothers," Carlos said. The trap door was covered back up. Everyone got into one of the brothers' car and drove off. On the way, Carlos told Matthew that whenever he visits, there are lookouts posted as a precaution. After driving for an hour they arrived at Carlos' house outside of town. Matthew was introduced to Carlos' wife and children. He would have to wait until morning to meet the grandmother. She was sleeping. Carlos told his family about Matthew. They talked and talked before retiring for the night.

The next morning everyone was up by nine o'clock and eating breakfast. Grandmother and the kids were up earlier, and had already eaten. The kids were outside playing, and Grandma was in her room.

After breakfast, Carlos and Matthew walked down a short hallway to Grandmother's room. The door was opened, but before they entered, Carlos stopped. "Before we go in, Matthew, I should warn you that she may not talk to you. When meeting someone for the first time, if she doesn't feel comfortable with them, she remains silent. If she does talk to you, that may mean she sees something in you that she likes."

When they entered the room, Matthew was taken back in time. Grandmother looked like the old Apache women in the pictures at the trading post. Carlos introduced her to Matthew. She said nothing. Carlos spoke in Spanish telling her how

Matthew had saved his life.

Then she spoke to Carlos in Chiricahua. Matthew could only guess that she was asking questions about him. When they had finished talking, she looked at Matthew.

"You saved my grandson's life. That makes you closer than brothers; you two have a special bond. You will always be welcome here. My family will always be thankful. I know we will see each other again."

Carlos and Matthew left the room. "She likes you," Carlos said.

They stayed another week. During their stay, Matthew felt like he was more part of this family than any foster home he had lived in.

They returned back across the border the same way they came, staying at different cousins' houses on the way.

When they started into the Pedregosa Mountains, Matthew suddenly stopped.

"What's wrong?" asked Carlos.

"Nothing, I was just curious. Is everyone your cousin?"

"Not everybody," answered Carlos laughing out loud. Ten days later they were back in the Gila Wilderness.

LEARNING TO SURVIVE

Spring was finally here, warm and windy. Since their return from Mexico, Carlos had never stopped teaching Matthew the ways of survival. He learned which plants were edible: cactus apples, mesquite beans, yucca stalks, cactus flowers, and seeds from the barrel cactus could all be eaten, just to name a few. Carlos showed Matthew how to prepare these plants.

He also learned how to track, hunt, fish, and to observe the movements of birds and animals. Carlos told him that this was Mother Nature's way of communicating in the wilderness. Throughout his teachings, Carlos, more than once, told him that everything he needed to survive was all around him. All he had to was open his eyes and mind.

He was taught how to make anything he would need, such as his own bow and arrows. The bow was made out of a piece of mulberry branch, cut and whittled into shape. His arrows were made out of cane or willow from along the river banks. The arrowheads were obsidian or certain other kinds of rocks; they were made using a deer antler as a tool. The arrow feathers were from a turkey.

Carlos and Matthew bow-hunted so as not to attract attention. They killed only what they needed: deer, elk, and turkey. Rabbits and other smaller game were trapped in snares; the meat was dried and cut into strips for jerky, or eaten fresh. The meat could be frozen in the winter. The fresh meat could be prepared in a stew consisting of yucca stocks and pods from the prickly pear cactus. Mesquite beans were also used, but these had to be cooked for a long time. Everything was cooked over an open pit or boiled in cans or pots; Carlos had gathered cans and cast-iron pots from the old abandoned mines.

Matthew learned to start fires using the fire drill or the fire bow method. Two sticks, twelve to fifteen inches long, were used in the fire drill method. One stick with a small notch was put on the ground, the other stick was pointed at one end. The point was placed into the notch. A handful of fine dry grass was placed around the notch. The pointed stick was twirled between the hands until the dry grass was ignited from the friction.

Like the fire drill method, the bow method uses two sticks. The bow method is like it sounds: placing a string from one end of a small branch to the other end, making a small bow. A loop is made around the pointed stick that fits into the notch. The bow is pushed and pulled back and forth until the dry fine grass ignites; Carlos and Matthew also started fires using flint.

In the months that followed, Matthew was taken to all the camps and springs throughout the mountains. Every three or four days they would move between camps. Carlos showed Matthew how to construct small temporary camps to be used when hiking between permant camps. These camps would be disassembled when they left. Carlos didn't like leaving any sign of activity behind. Matthew couldn't believe how isolated the main camps were. Not only that, but there were no visible signs of access. The camps were scattered throughout northern New Mexico and northern Arizona. Some of the camps were natural caves used by Carlos' Apache ancestors; other camps were old abandoned mines. Old mines were dangerous, but Carlos had re-enforced them. If Matthew had not been with Carlos, he never would have found them. A person could walk by them and never know it. Matthew, now more than ever, could understand why Carlos would never be found.

One afternoon they stopped in front of three old mines. Underneath the thick brush in front of two of the old mines, were rock graves. "Did they die at the hands of the Apaches or other miners? Maybe they were victims of the wilderness. What do you think?" asked Matthew.

"We'll never know. Before we go to where we will stay tonight, I want to show you a special place."

Above the mines they began climbing higher and higher until they reached the very top.

"Up here, I feel as if I could almost touch the sky. It's the most beautiful place in the mountains. I've spent a lot of time here watching the white clouds slowly passing by. Like them, I wish I could move about freely and not stay hidden from everyone. Sometimes I pretend I'm one of the clouds. Up here, I can escape from reality. This is the only place where I feel free. Here, at times, I feel closer to God than if I was in church. Matthew, if something happens to me, if I don't return to my family in Mexico, promise me that you'll bring me up here. Bury me deep and pile the rocks high. I don't want the predators to dig me up; I don't want to be part of nature's food chain." Carlos then let out a short laugh and then they both laughed.

"I promise," said Matthew.

On the way back to camp, Carlos and Matthew were atop one of the high mountain peaks. Carlos was showing Matthew how to descend through the arroyo below them.

"One important thing you must learn about hiking through the wilderness is to look over the terrain that's around you and in front of you. Remember the mountain peaks and rocky outcroppings. Use them for reference points. Know the areas where you can hike through. There will be areas that are impassable, places where the mesquite and brush is so thick that you can't penetrate. Use the game trails if you know where they go. There are no trails to any of my hidden camps. You'll have to remember where every camp is and how to find them.

"If you're ever in a situation where you hear or see someone else hiking, you may not want to be seen. Retreat into your surroundings, and then freeze. It will be your movement that would catch their eye. Animals in the wilderness freeze when they sense danger. We could be looking right at them and not know it."

Looking further down the arroyo, they could barley see two hikers climbing up one of the other mountains.

"There shouldn't be any one else up here. It's too far off of any trail. The side of that mountain is nothing but smooth slippery rocks and mesquites. Those hikers wouldn't be up there unless they had a reason," said Carlos.

Still watching them, Carlos said to Matthew, "Let's get out of here. I don't want to be seen. They might be looking for me."

Carlos turned around and started leaving. Matthew yelled, "One of them just fell!"

Carlos quickly turned back around saw the hiker falling down the mountain side. The other hiker hurriedly started climbing down toward the other one, slipping, and sliding, before eventually falling and landing near the first hiker.

As Matthew and Carlos watched, the first hiker to fall moved his arms, but otherwise remained still. The second hiker slowly got up and limped over to help the other one.

"They need help," said Carlos. "You know I can't go down there. If I was by myself I would have to. But you're here and you can help them. You know I would if I could."

"I know," said Matthew. "You head back to camp and I'll take care of them."

Carlos left for camp wishing he could help them, but knew it was best not to stay and help. Matthew started hiking down below. It took him some time before he finally reached them.

Panicking and crying, a young lady saw Matthew. "I'm glad to see someone. My dad thinks his back is broken. We're both cut and scraped-up. My arm hurts and my ankle is badly sprained or broken. Luckily, my cell phone still works. I've called for help. A rescue party is on its way. I couldn't tell them exactly how to get here. I'm scared. I hope my father is going to be all right, I sure hope the rescue party can find us. I don't dare call my mom; she'd be worried to death."

"Calm down. Stop crying," said Matthew. "Everything's going to be all right. I'll go down and meet the rescue party. You stay here with your dad and talk to him until we return."

Matthew started hiking down the mountain to the trail below. Once he was on the trail, he looked for the rescue party. Before he saw them he heard the helicopter. "I hope Carlos is out of sight," he said to himself.

Matthew met the rescuers. "There's no place for the helicopter to land. They'll have to bring the hikers out on stretchers."

Matthew guided them up the mountain until they reached the father and daughter. Matthew stepped aside and let everyone go in front of him. Unnoticed, he disappeared into the mountains and hiked back to join Carlos at camp.

A week had passed since Carlos had shown Matthew the locations of the different camps. One morning as they were drinking coffee, Carlos said, "I think you're ready to go out on your own. What do you think?"

"That's the way I feel," answered Matthew.

"You know all the mountains and arroyos that we've been to. But there is one area I've never taken you to. It's located about five miles west of here. We've passed by it   many times, but never explored it. I myself avoid it; you must also avoid it. I'll tell you why: After my friend drove me across the border, I made my way through Arizona and into New Mexico. When I first entered the New Mexico wilderness looking for a cave to stay in, I finally found one. It looked like it hadn't been occupied in a while. There were small animal as well as large animal bones scattered among the pieces of hide, fur, and feathers. There were dried feces of different animals scattered everywhere.

"I enclosed the cave by stacking rocks from floor to ceiling. This would protect me from the animals. There was a small entrance that I sealed during the day when I was out hunting. It was also sealed at night. I kept a fire going during the night to discourage any visitors.

"One night I heard some kind of an animal outside the cave. I built the fire up high and grabbed my spear just in case. I placed the tip into the fire. I also had made torches for lighting up the cave, and I placed one of these into the fire.

"All of a sudden some of the rocks tumbled into the cave. It was a black bear. He stuck his head into the opening, growling and knocking in more rocks. The fire between us kept him at bay.

"I grabbed the flaming torch and shoved it into his face and neck. The bear let out a painful sound. I could smell the burning fur and flesh. He was swiping at his face and the flaming torch, trying to get rid of the pain and fire. But still the bear wasn't ready to back off.

"I kept jabbing at him with the torch. Then I threw the torch aside and grabbed my spear with both hands. I pushed it as hard as I could right into the bear's eye. Blood began pouring out of his eye. The terrible sounds he made were of pain and anger. Reluctantly, he backed off, turned around, and left.

"After I built the wall back up, I stayed awake the rest of the night. The next morning I followed his tracks and some splatters of blood into the area that I am warning you about.

"That bear is still out there. I know because I've seen him a few times. Now he has only one eye. Sometimes when I'm moving between camps, not even near his area, I have the feeling he's following me. He could be waiting for the right time and opportunity to kill me. If it was a grizzly bear it would have killed me that night. A grizzly never would have given up. Avoid this area and be careful at all times. The bear might think you are me and kill you. Tomorrow you'll be going out by yourself for the first time."

"Tell me about your first time out alone," said Matthew.

"My father had taught me and my two brothers the Apache way of survival in the wilderness. We started learning at a very young age. The two things we needed that we always took along were our knives and a piece of flint for starting a fire. We knew the primitive Apache way. The flint-starting was the easiest and fastest.

"Our weeks were taken up by going to school and helping around the house. Our weekends, however, were different from that of most boys our age: We were taken out into the wilderness almost every weekend.

"We were taught everything from hunting, making weapons, tracking, and finding water when there was none visible. We learned which plants were edible and how to prepare them. We learned everything we needed to know to survive.

"Two things my dad told us that we should never forget: survival is mental, and when in the wilderness, you have to become a part of the wilderness in order to survive.

"When I was twelve years old, my dad took me out like he had many times before. But this time it would be different. He blindfolded me, and then stood in front of me and said, 'Put your hands on my shoulders. Follow me, and don't be afraid. Fear can be your worst enemy. You must feel safe, even in the darkness. Feel and know what type of terrain is beneath your feet. Smell and touch the surrounding bushes as they brush against us. Listen to the sound of the wilderness. Picture in your mind what you see and feel.'

"When we were near a river or stream, I heard the sound of the moving water. 'How far away is it?' my dad would ask.

"When we stopped to camp, my blindfold didn't come off until after dark. Before dark I would just sit. He would walk around and tell me to listen to the sounds he made walking through the bushes. 'Be able to tell if I'm coming closer, or going farther away,' he said.

"This went on for three days and two nights. The third night he told me that when I awoke in the morning, he would be gone. I would have to find my way back alone.

"'Remember the sounds you've heard, and everything you experienced in your world of darkness. Remember everything you learned about survival. If you can do this you will have no trouble finding your way home,' he said. We said goodnight.

"When I awoke the next morning, I looked over to where he was sleeping. He was gone.

"All he left me with were the clothes I was wearing and my knife. I was alone and on my own.

"I remembered that when we hiked into the mountains, the sun was always at my back. I needed to hike out facing into the sun. Now I knew which direction to go.

"We had camped in a flat sandy area. I started looking for any signs that my father might have left. He would not intentionally leave any, but he always said that you can find some sort of a sign if you look hard enough. I looked and looked, but found nothing.

"Then I had an idea. I climbed up on the flat rocks that sloped down to the sandy area. I walked around the edge of the rocks looking down. I saw something there that didn't belong. In among the many rabbit and bird tracks, was a small half circle in the sand where the sand and rock merged together. It was the back edge of his boot heel. He left it when he stepped up from the sand onto the rock. Now I knew in which direction he had left.

"I hiked all morning finding a partial print every now and then. I checked bushes for broken branches that would tell me if I was going the right way. Some of the branches were broken in both directions. This told me the way we had come in and the way he had left.

"By late afternoon I was hungry. I ate wild berries and what are called cactus apples. The red apple-looking fruit is very nutritious, but covered with hair-like stickers. You remove them with a handful of brush. Brush off the stickers, peel and then eat.

"I stopped when I heard the sound of running water. It was the same sound I had heard before when I was blindfolded. I found the stream and drank.

"Before dark I scouted around and found a rabbit trail. I could tell by the many prints that it had been used often. I set one snare, walked a ways farther down the trail, and then set another. The next morning I checked my two snares; I had caught a rabbit in one of them.

"I started a fire by striking the flint against my steel knife. I cleaned and cooked individual pieces over the fire on the end of a stick. I ate what I needed, then rationed the rest to provide me until I reached home. Two and a half days later I was standing in my front yard.

"As I approached the house I could see my father sitting on the front porch. He looked up when I stepped onto the porch.

"'What took you so long?' he asked, and then smiled."

Matthew was so inspired by Carlos' story he hardly slept that night.

Early the next morning Matthew was eager to go out on his own. He could only take his knife, per Carlos. When Matthew first started going out, he would be gone three or four days at a time. Then he started staying out a week at a time. He was taught to count the days by the sunsets. One time he stayed out three weeks before returning to camp. When he returned from his last outing, Carlos had just finished making a fire.

"You're just in time for some venison steak. I killed a deer a couple of days ago. You know, when we first talked, you told me that you thought that you belonged in the mountains. I also think you belong out here. In fact, I know it. There are not many men   that could live out here alone. When I was teaching you, I could tell everything came as second nature to you. You have that instinct for survival that most people will never feel or ever know. You could survive in any situation."

"Thanks," replied Matthew. "I feel so natural living out here. Not seeing another person, except now and then, is enough for me. It doesn't bother me being alone."

"Your kind is few and far between," said Carlos. "You want to live out here alone. But for me, I have no choice. I am forced to live out here alone."

Matthew and Carlos would separate for weeks at a time, routinely re-supplying their camps. Before they separated, they would always decide when and where to meet again. They kept track of the days between meets by counting the sunsets. Carlos stayed higher in the mountains and was never seen. Matthew, staying out of sight, would scout out the hiking trails, checking on the activity of the hikers, campers, and hunters.

The only time he was ever seen was when he would be on the lower trail to the Post; the lower trails were popular with the hikers.

Whenever Matthew met someone he would greet them. Now and then, he would come across hikers needing help.

Some of them were novices. Matthew could tell novice hikers right-off by their gear: Their outfits were the newest and most colorful from head to toe. They also carried more supplies than Bill sold at the Post. They were usually exhausted and confused as to which trail they were on.

The two questions that he would always be asked were,

"How much farther?" and "Does it get any easier up ahead?" After Matthew answered them, some would turn around, but others kept going. After one such encounter, making sure he wasn't followed, he headed back to camp. Wanting to do some exploring, he hiked back in a different direction. Hiking up an arroyo that turned into a dead end, he decided to climb up and out onto the top. A quick movement caught his eye. It was a fox. He watched the fox come out of a hole, scamper away, and disappear into the underbrush and rocks. Matthew's attention went back to the hole in the side of the bank.

Matthews's curiosity got the best of him. Cautiously, he approached the hole. He knelt down and looked in as far as he could see. Then he threw some small rocks into the opening. This would let him know if there were rattlesnakes or any other animals inside. Hearing no sound, he knew it was safe to take a closer look. Matthew saw something inside. He enlarged the opening and then crawled inside. What a surprise! There were four bows and plenty of arrows. The arrow feathers were all but gone — probably chewed by varmints. The arrowheads themselves were what really caught his eye. They were tarnished copper, but otherwise, they were perfect. There were also six old rifles and plenty of ammunition. Any metal on the rifles was rusted and the ammunition corroded beyond use. Everything was ruined by the rain that had leaked in over the years. Any food that had been stored was ruined by the dampness, or eaten by varmints. Not seeing anything else, he crawled back out. He couldn't wait to tell Carlos what he had found. Matthew covered the opening and then returned to camp.

"That was a cache. It was where the Apaches would hide their supplies, including their weapons. Caches like the one you found were located throughout Apacheria, homeland of the Apaches. If their camp was attacked and they had to escape, what was left behind was either taken or destroyed. From the cache they could re-supply themselves."

Matthew then asked Carlos about the copper arrowheads.

"They were made by the Chihene Apaches, also known as the Coppermine Apaches. Arrows with the copper points could penetrate anything. When sharpened, they were like razor blades."

"Did you cover the cache?" asked Carlos.

"Of course."

"Good, if anyone discovered it, there would be people up here looking for anything and everything."

Two days later the early morning brought the smell of smoke. Carlos looked northeast and saw thick smoke.

"How far away is it?" asked Matthew.

"It's about three miles or more," answered Carlos. "Maybe it's at one of the campgrounds. It's no threat to us yet, but that's not what I am worried about. Before long, the mountains will be full of forestry officials, firefighters, and law enforcement.

"It's monsoon season. Maybe the rain will help them in putting out the fire. We can't take a chance on being seen. Let's play it safe and go back down to Mexico. By the time we return, maybe the fire will be out."

They stayed in Mexico three weeks. Matthew spent more time with Grandmother than anyone else. He liked hearing her stories about the culture and the stories of individual Chiricahua that were part of history, though her stories can't be found in any history books. Like Carlos' survival lessons, her stories were also of survival, but survival of the Chiricahua people.

While on their return trip in Arizona, Carlos showed Matthew locations where his ancestors had hidden and camped, places they used after they had left the San Carlos Indian Reservation on their way to raid in Mexico.

A WINTER ALONE

When Matthew and Carlos were across the state line into New Mexico, Matthew went to the Post for supplies. Carlos hiked ahead to one of their camps. He and Carlos would meet at the camp, which was three days into the wilderness.

Bill was glad to see Matthew. "When I don't see you for a while, I worry." Bill said.

"No need to worry. Most of the time I'm with the mountain man."

"That makes me feel better," said Bill. Matthew asked Bill about the forest fire.

"The fire was started by a careless camper."

"That's what the mountain man thought might have happened," said Matthew. After trading for supplies, Matthew left and headed to camp.

He had been hiking for about three hours, when he headed up a mountain to a game trail. After another hour, he left the trail and started hiking up the mountain. Something moved in the rocks in front of him. Matthew stopped. "There shouldn't be anyone up here," he said to himself. It could only be an animal. He readied his bow and slowly started approaching the rocks. To his surprise, a voice yelled out,

"It's only me!" Matthew lowered his bow as Carlos stepped out from behind the rocks.

"What are you doing, Carlos?" Matthew yelled. "I could have killed you."

"I wouldn't have let you kill me. That's why I yelled. Expect the unexpected. Be prepared for anything," answered Carlos.

Matthew looked at him and smiled. "Just for that, you're the cook tonight."

Carlos laughed, "You really trust my cooking?" he said. They stayed at a temporary camp that night.

Three days later they arrived in a main camp located in an abandoned mine. The monsoon season was close to being over. The daytime and nighttime temperatures were slowly dropping; cooler days and colder nights would soon change to colder days and freezing nights. It would be snowing before long.

While sitting around the campfire, drinking coffee Carlos asked Matthew if he was going with him to Mexico this winter.

"I think I'll stay here. It'll be my first winter I spend alone," Matthew answered.

"There will be times when you'll be snowed in, but all the camps are well-stocked for the winter. You'll have everything you need."

"I know. I might even go down lower where it's a little warmer and not as much snow," said Matthew.

"My first winter up here, I moved between camps whenever the weather would permit. Sometimes I would have to stay in one location for a week or more, cold and snowy all winter long. During one of these stays of isolation, for the first time since I had been in these mountains, I became lonely and depressed. All I thought about was my family. That was my first Christmas without them. It's that time of year when my family and all our friends get together to celebrate the holidays. There was nothing I could do to change my situation. I made it through that winter by remembering past Christmases. That's the last winter I spent up here. Now, as you know, I go to Mexico. I'm going to leave earlier than usual this year. I want to visit a cousin in northern Arizona," said Carlos.

Three weeks later, Carlos left for Arizona. Matthew went with him until they were off the mountain. There they separated. Before Carlos had gone very far, he turned and yelled, "Matthew, I hope you make it through the winter!" Matthew could see the smile on Carlos' face. Matthew yelled back "Don't worry about me; I had a good teacher. You just worry about getting caught!"

Carlos waved good-bye. Matthew watched him until he was out of sight. Matthew then went back to camp. During the following weeks it had become colder. Matthew spent his time hunting and bringing in firewood to different camps. The camps were well supplied, but it's smart to overstock for winter. He stayed in each camp for one or two weeks. Looking at the sky one morning, he knew there was a snow storm coming in. It would be the first one of the year.

He was camped in a natural cave that had been used by the Apaches many years ago. It was so concealed that if Carlos hadn't taken him to it, he never would have found it. In fact, about a month later, Matthew went back and had a hard time locating it.

Matthew was sitting by the fire finishing his evening meal and drinking a cup of coffee. "I wonder where Carlos is," he asked himself. "He's probably in Mexico," he decided.

Before he called it a night, he walked over to the rocks piled up at the cave's entrance. He could see between the rocks. It had started to snow.

The next morning when he awoke, he put more wood on the fire to get the chill off the air. He looked out between the rocks. It was still snowing. It snowed off and on for the next two weeks. Between snows, he hunted for fresh meat and brought in more firewood. The firewood was wet, but inside the warm cave, it will dry eventually. He had plenty of dry firewood, but bringing in more, gives him something to do.

Matthew had just finished his afternoon meal of stew, consisting of chunks of deer meat and dried yucca flowers, and was sitting around the fire keeping warm. While chewing on a piece of jerky he started thinking about how different he felt since rescuing Carlos. He tried to come up with an explanation, but was at a loss. One thing for certain: besides being his mentor, Carlos had become the closet friend he's ever had. Actually, Carlos was his first real friend.

One thing that wasn't much different, but had changed somewhat, were his childhood dreams. They were still there, but not as vivid and didn't reoccur as frequently. Maybe in time they would disappear completely.

Matthew spent the rest of the winter moving between camps, never seeing anyone. A lot of the campgrounds were closed for the winter. Also, the cold winter kept people out of the mountains. It was freezing cold all winter long with very little rain. Three times he was snowed-in for a week or more.

With winter ending and snow starting to melt, Matthew decided to go to the Post. He could trade what he had made during the winter.

It hadn't snowed for a week and a half. It was time for Matthew to head out of the higher elevation and work his way down below. He planned on leaving in the morning; but Mother Nature had plans of her own: It started snowing.

"I'll just stay in this old mine where I can be nice and warm," he said to himself. It snowed all day, heavy at times and a little windy. It had finally stopped by nightfall. When Matthew woke up at night to put more wood on the fire, he looked outside and saw it was snowing again.

The snow had stopped by morning. It was clear and cold, but otherwise a nice day. Matthew left early. Before long, he would be on the trail below. If it was summer, he might see a hiker in the area now and then. But this was winter, and very few were out hiking.

Matthew had been hiking down from the snow-covered mountains for about an hour. Something in the snow caught his eye. It was footprints. He was barley able to follow them until he came to an area where the prints were more distinct. Still, they were almost covered. There were two sets, one a little smaller than the other. The two sets must belong to a man and a woman; a child's footprint would be a lot smaller than any of these. He followed them a little farther. He could tell by the direction they were going that whoever belonged to those tracks were lost. The tracks led Matthew in circles.

In some places they doubled back and crisscrossed. Eventually, the tracks went straight ahead through some bushes. All the bushes were completely covered with snow, except one. Three or four of the branches were bent and broken. The green foliage was slightly exposed. Matthew looked closer. He could tell the breaks were fresh. Someone had grabbed this bush for a reason. He looked down at the prints and saw that the smaller prints were distorted. The woman had slipped and grabbed the bush for support. It had happened this morning, judging by the disturbance of the snow on the broken branches. Also, the ground was showing where the woman had slipped. Beyond that spot, the prints went forward and backward. Maybe two people were out taking a morning hike, but Matthew didn't think so. He was still too high up in the mountains. There were no hiking trails and he had never seen anyone this high in the mountains, especially during the winter.

Looking up ahead, he already knew where the tracks would lead him. There was an outcropping of rocks with only one place for shelter. If there was anyone still out here, that's where they would be. As Matthew got closer, he yelled, "Hello!"
Right away someone answered back.

Matthew made his way over to them. Two people were huddled together behind the rocks, trying to keep warm. No fire.

"We're freezing to death", said the man. The woman was so cold, she was shaking.

"We're glad to see someone," she said.

Matthew took off his heavy coat and placed it around both of them.

"First thing I'm going to do is build you a fire."

"Everything's wet and covered with snow. How are you going to build a fire?" the man asked.

"Among the rocks underneath the overhang, there is shelter where the small varmints stay. There are always small dry branches and brush. There should be some dry branches at the bottom of the piles. If I have to use wet branches, I can strip off the wet bark. Then I can whittle down to the dry part of the branch.

"I'm going to take care of you and lead you out of here. You're going to be all right." He then gave them some food and water, and then built a fire. They started warming up and introduced themselves as Fred and Carol Parkins. Matthew also introduced himself.

"What are you doing up here?" Fred asked.

"I live up here."

"What are you two doing up here?" Matthew asked back before they had a chance to ask any more questions. "This is no place to be, especially in the winter."

"We live down in Silver City. Yesterday we decided to take a drive and go for a hike. I have a four-wheel-drive truck. We took Highway 180 out of Silver City. Once we were in the mountains, we found a dirt road and followed it. The scenery was so beautiful we stayed on it. In the afternoon, when it started lightly snowing, we decided to stop and take a short walk. We hadn't gone too far from the truck. We were just enjoying ourselves in the snow. It started snowing heavier, so we decided to go back to the truck. The wind picked up and the snow started blowing. We couldn't see very far at first, and then we couldn't see at all through the blowing snow. We thought we were heading back to the truck, but somehow, we got turned around and became lost. We kept trying to find the truck. We knew it would be dark soon, so we found these rocks and stayed here all night. We have been cold and wet all night long.

"I tried my cell phone, but there was no signal. We're not campers or hunters, so I don't know that much about building fires, other than using a match," said Fred.

"We went out this morning, but were afraid that we might get lost even more, so we came back here," said Mary.

"I know. I saw where you had slipped and grabbed the bush. Then you turned around and headed back here." Matthew said. Both Fred and Carol looked at him with amazement.

"I'm going to find your truck."

"I have a good idea as to where you left your truck: There's only one dirt road near here. It's really not that far away. While I am gone dry your clothes. Take off your boots and dry your socks. Dry your boots as best you can." Matthew left.

After not even thirty minutes of hiking, he saw the truck down below.

"They have a four-wheel-drive. They won't have a problem getting back to the main road," Matthew thought to himself.

Actually, they were only about four hundred yards away from the truck, but Matthew knew that anyone could become disoriented and lost in the wilderness. It happens summer or winter.

Matthew brought them back to their truck. He waited to make sure it started. The couple sat in the truck with the heater on, warming up the truck as well as themselves. After a few minutes, they got out of the truck to thank Matthew, but he was already gone. They looked around and called his name, but there was no answer.

Matthew had disappeared back into the wilderness. Before long, he was on the trail leading to the Post. The trail was free of snow, but muddy. It would be a couple more weeks before the trail would be completely dry. He hadn't been on the trail for very long when he heard conversation in the distance. Heading toward him, was a young couple wearing back packs. They came to an abrupt stop when they saw Matthew.

"We're sure glad to see someone. I think we're lost. Is this the trail to the lower camps?" the man asked.

"No, you are going higher into the mountains. There are no camps up there. The trail ends a short distance just ahead. Go back down about a mile. There's a sign showing the locations of the lower camps."

"Thanks," they both said, and then headed back down the trail.

Matthew shook his head. "It won't be long before there will be a lot of hikers and campers just like them up here," Matthew said to himself.

Later in the day, Matthew arrived at the Post. As always, Bill was glad to see him. They talked and traded. When they were finished, Matthew headed back into the mountains. He followed the trail until almost dark, and then hiked straight up the mountain.

A temporary camp was located on a high ledge enclosed by rocks and brush. The enclosure was cold inside. The first thing Matthew did was build a fire. He sat by the fire until he fell asleep, waking up every so often to put more wood on the fire.

The next morning he awoke at sunrise. He thought about how quiet the wilderness was early in the morning. The only sounds were those of birds. He liked to think that they were waking up the rest of the forest.

He left before noon. Two days later, he arrived at the camp from where he and Carlos had departed. He was disappointed that Carlos wasn't there. A week passed by, but still no Carlos. Matthew was beginning to worry. Maybe he had been caught. No, that couldn't be. I don't know why I should worry. I'm sure he's all right."

Carlos arrived two days later.

"I wondered what had happened to you."

"Why, were you worried about me?"

"Not at all," answered Matthew. "Well, maybe a little." They both laughed.

It was the start of spring. Late in the morning Matthew was hiking in a new and different mountain range east of where he and Carlos were camped.

For Matthew, the whole experience of hiking and exploring was an adventure.

The arroyo that he was hiking came to a dead end because of the high thick mesquites. It was impossible for him to get through them. Matthew climbed up the side of the arroyo and looked on the other side of the mesquites. The arroyo continued, almost concealing what looked like an old trail. He hiked down to the bottom of the arroyo. It was obvious by the brush that had grown on the trail, that hadn't been used in years. He followed the trail for about an hour. Twice he had to use flat rock steps where the trail ascended abruptly. Matthew could tell that the steps had been placed by someone years ago. Looking up ahead he saw that the trail went upward. He suspected that it went to the three large boulders at the very top of the mountain. It took him another hour to reach the top. The path stopped at the base of the boulders.

He was excited and confused at what he saw. It's some kind of scratching or markings on the rocks. There were pictures of animals, people, squares, circles, and other images. He climbed to the top of one of the three large boulders. The tops were also covered with the strange markings.

Before he left he took another look at the boulders. "How old are these markings? Who did this? What does all this mean?" Matthew asked himself.

He hiked out of the arroyo and back to camp.

He hadn't even had a chance to sit down, when Carlos asked,

"What did you find? I can tell by the look on your face that you found something."

Matthew told him about finding the foot path and the drawings on the rocks.

"Those are called petroglyphs. They were made by Native Americans centuries ago.

Petroglyphs are picture records of events that happened in the past. We don't know the meaning of some, but others are obvious. They were made by pounding on the rock," Carlos told him.

The next day Matthew and Carlos hiked back to the site.

Carlos explained to Matthew the figures that he knew about.

They stayed a little longer at the site before they began hiking around the boulders and down the other side of the mountain.

Matthew could tell that Carlos was looking for something else.

Underneath the thick brush, and almost completely covered, were flat rocks. The brush growing in the cracks almost hid what Carlos was looking for.

"I knew there had to be an old Indian camp close by. Look at the grinding holes in the rocks, Matthew."

They could see twenty or thirty grinding holes. They knew this was a large camp.

"The petroglyphs and this old Indian camp are good examples of many places that the wilderness keeps hidden. Places like this should stay that way."

Finding nothing else, they returned to camp.

THE WOLF

The weather was hot, and windy with occasional rain to cool things down. This year the monsoon season started a few weeks earlier than normal, but that's not unusual. Carlos and Matthew were camped high in the mountains. Carlos left early in the morning to check one of the springs higher in the mountains. He would be gone until the next day. Matthew was going to leave later that same morning to check the two snares he had set the day before. He would return to camp that same day. As he was leaving, Matthew could see more storm clouds forming; a storm would start later that evening.

It wouldn't take long to check the two snares—they weren't too far from camp. The first snare hadn't been triggered, but the second one had snared a rabbit; that would be dinner. After he reset the snare, Matthew headed back to camp. He wanted to be there before the storm hit.

The storm started after dark. There was plenty of lightning, thunder, and rain. It rained heavy at times, and then stopped completely. In between rains, Matthew stepped outside the mine. He liked the fresh clean smell of the air after the rain. While outside, he kept hearing a whining sound. It would start, and then stop again. It sounded like a wolf. "Maybe it was injured," he thought to himself. Matthew went back into the mine and lay down next to the fire.

The storm lasted throughout the night. The next morning the sun was out. The storm had passed on through and headed east. Matthew stepped outside to take in the warmth of the morning sun before breakfast. Once again, he heard the whining. After a breakfast of left-over rabbit and jerky, he decided to investigate the whining sound.

He followed the sound; the closer he got the louder the whining became. Not knowing what to expect, he made himself ready with his bow. If the wolf was hurt, he would be very dangerous; he might even attack. With caution, Matthew approached the whining sound. The sound suddenly stopped. Matthew saw nothing in front of him, but knew he had been spotted. He froze, and then slowly moved his head from left to right. He knew that if the wolf attacked, his reflexes would have to be quick and his aim accurate. The wolf would have the advantage.

Then he saw it. Underneath the bush lay a wolf pup.

Carlos had told him that there were a few Mexican gray wolves in eastern Arizona and western New Mexico. Matthew had heard them howling sometimes at night, but never had seen one.

The pup wasn't moving, but just lying there, not taking his eyes off Matthew. It looked to be about two months old, but Matthew didn't really know how old the wolf was.

He had no idea how long the pup had been laying there. Maybe he was hurt. Looking at the mud around him, Matthew couldn't see any paw prints. Something must have happened to the mother; she would not have abandoned her pup.

Matthew crawled through the mud, brush, and mesquites. As he got closer, the pup rose up on all fours and began growling.

Matthew pulled a piece of jerky from his pocket and threw it down in front of the pup. It seemed like an hour passed before the pup cautiously approached the jerky. Finally, he gobbled it down, and then looked up at Matthew.

"Poor little fellow's hungry." He threw him another piece. The pup came closer, but not too close. Matthew looked at the pup.

"I have to go back to camp, maybe you'll be all right, maybe not. I've done all I can do for you," Matthew said.

Matthew crawled back out, and started to leave. The pup began to follow. Matthew looked at the pup, and then said to him, "I can't leave you here. I guess you had better come with me. You have no mother; you're an orphan like me."

Matthew took a closer look at the pup. It was a male with a large head and large paws.

"You're going to be a big one.

"If you're going to stay with me I'll have to give you a name. Matthew thought for a minute and then said, "Because of the storm last night, I'll call you 'Thunder.'"

Finally, they reached the camp. Thunder ate some more, drank some water, lay down, and fell asleep. Matthew smiled and said, "Carlos is sure going to be surprised when he gets back."

When Thunder awoke, he looked around. He saw Matthew and went right over and sat directly in front of him. Matthew knew what he wanted: He wondered if Thunder would take the jerky from his hand. Before Matthew reached out very far, Thunder pulled it from his fingers.

"Good boy."

Suddenly, Thunder turned around and started growling and barking at something off in the distance. Matthew saw Carlos coming. As Carlos entered the camp, Thunder would not stop barking and growling.

"Its okay boy, he's our friend."

It was only after Matthew walked over to Carlos and they started talking, that Thunder stopped.

"What the heck is this?" asked Carlos.

"It's a wolf."

"I know that, but what's he doing here?"

Matthew explained to Carlos how he had found him.

"We don't need a wolf," said Carlos.

"He can warn us of danger, or let us know when people are too close."

"All the time I've lived in the wilderness I've never needed a wolf to warn me of anything. If you want him to stay, Matthew, he's your wolf. You take care of him."

Matthew turned to Thunder. "Did you hear that, boy? I've never even had a dog, and now I have a pet wolf. This is great! Thanks Carlos. I can't wait to tell Bill I have a pet wolf."

It was Matthew's turn to cook dinner. He was so happy and busy preparing the meal that he hadn't paid much attention to anything else. When he looked around to see what Carlos was doing and where Thunder was, he saw Carlos talking to Thunder.

Smiling and shaking his head, Matthew thought to himself, "There goes my pet wolf."

The three of them were together a lot, but most of the time, it was just Matthew and Thunder out, constantly hiking and exploring.

By the end of summer, Thunder knew where all the camps were. And by now he had grown into a big, strong wolf. Thunder was not only Matthew's faithful companion, but also his protector.

There was one time that Matthew would never forget. They were descending a mountain. The footing was slippery because of loose rocks. When he put his weight on a rock to test its stability, it slipped out from under him. Down he went. He slid down the mountain of loose rocks for about ten or eleven feet before coming to a stop on solid ground. Matthew was unhurt.

When he started to pull himself up using the rock next to him for support, Thunder barked twice, alerting Matthew. Matthew froze, hardly breathing. Right above Matthews's head, almost out of his sight on the rock, was a rattlesnake, coiled, and ready to strike. After what seemed like an eternity, Matthew began very slowly to inch his body back down to the ground. Laying flat on his back, he began edging down away from the rock. When Matthew was eight or nine feet below, and knowing he was safe enough, he stood up. After letting out a huge sigh of relief, Matthew gave Thunder a big hug.

"Thanks, Thunder. You saved my life!"

The days were becoming cooler, but still nice. There were still plenty of hikers and the campgrounds were still full. The campers wanted to get in their last outing before winter. After they're all gone, the wilderness restores itself.

Matthew and Thunder had been out checking their camps, making sure every camp was well-supplied for the winter.

"It's time to head back to our main camp. Carlos is waiting for us, Thunder." Thunder looked at Matthew as if understanding every word he said. Then Thunder barked.

"You understand me better than most people I've ever met. I never had a dog. It's said that a dog is man's best friend, but I think a wolf is a much better friend," Matthew said out loud.

Two nights had gone by, and now they were just a day away

from camp. They left early that morning, and would be in camp by nightfall. It was late afternoon and Thunder was leading the way. He had been this way so many times he knew the way home better than Matthew.

Matthew couldn't keep up, but he still had Thunder in sight. Thunder suddenly stopped and growled. When Matthew caught up to him, Thunder turned and barked once.

"What is it, Thunder?"

Looking at a clearing down below, he was taken by surprise.

He saw a young man carrying a small boy, and a young woman carrying a little girl. The boy and the woman were crying.

The woman turned to the man. He heard her ask him, "What are we going to do? We've been out here wandering around all afternoon. We're lost and are going to die out here."

"I'm sorry. I don't know what to do," answered the man.

Matthew watched them for a minute.

"Stay behind me," Matthew told Thunder. Then they made their way down towards the clearing. When they were close enough to be seen, Matthew yelled a hello.

When the couple saw him, they put the children down and both began yelling and waving their arms. When Matthew reached the clearing, the first thing the woman said was, "Thank God."

"We're lost," said the man.

Then instinctively, they grabbed the children and placed them behind themselves, keeping them from Matthew.

That's when Matthew realized that they had just seen Thunder.

"It's okay. That's my wolf, Thunder. He won't hurt you. How did you end up way out here in the middle of nowhere?"

"Wanting to be by ourselves, we camped in a secluded spot

outside the main camping area. This morning after breakfast, we decided to take a short walk. We weren't going to go very far. We took very little water and only a few snacks for the kids," said the woman.

"Maybe fifteen or twenty minutes had gone by when we decided to return to camp," said the man. "Somehow we got turned around, and have been lost ever since. We've spent all day trying to find our way back to camp. We're tired and hungry."

Matthew gave them some water and jerky. They introduced themselves and their kids.

"Take it easy on the water. Don't drink too fast. You're about half a day from the nearest main camp. It's too late to go back there today. In the morning I'll take you out of here. For now, I'll build a shelter and a fire. At night it can be colder up here than down below."

"I have some food and more water hidden not far from here. Thunder will stay with you while I'm gone. He'll protect you."

Looking at the couple, Matthew told them to gather the dry grass and put it down in the shelter for bedding and gather up more firewood. "We have to keep a fire going all night," he said. Matthew left and returned an hour later.

The kids were asleep with Thunder lying between the two of them.

"I know we wouldn't have survived if you hadn't seen us," said the husband.

"Don't thank me for finding you, thank Thunder. Thunder saw you and alerted me."

"We can't thank the both of you enough for saving our lives," added the wife.

"I hope you don't mind us asking, and we don't mean to pry,

but what are you doing out here in the mountains? You don't look like a hunter," said the husband.

"I live here with my wolf, Thunder. The wilderness is where we both live and belong."

"Once again, we want to thank you," said the husband.

"Glad we were of some help. I think we better get some sleep. Morning comes early," said Matthew.

The next morning after breakfast, Matthew took them down close to one of the main campgrounds.

"We know where we are now," said the wife.

"Come with us to our camp and I'll write you a check. We can never repay you enough, but I want to pay you something," the husband said.

"Money is no good to me out here. Living in the mountains is all I need. But there is one thing you can do for me: The trading post is not too far from here. The man who owns it is named is Bill. Tell him you saw me and that I'm all right. When he doesn't see me for awhile, he gets a little worried."

"Sure will," said the husband.

"We bought supplies from him the first day we got here," said the wife.

The family gave Matthew and Thunder good-bye hugs, and then watched as the man and his wolf headed back into the mountains until they were out of sight.

Winter was almost here. Carlos and Matthew could see a change in Thunder; he wasn't in camp as much, spending more time alone out in the wilderness, sometimes all day.

One day after he and Matthew had been out hiking, Thunder ran ahead of Matthew to the camp as usual. But when Matthew arrived at camp, there was no Thunder. Matthew looked and called for him until dark, but still no Thunder. Matthew wasn't worried. He knew Thunder could fend for himself. Well, maybe Matthew was a little worried.

When Matthew awoke the next morning, the first thing he did was to look over to where Thunder slept. Still no Thunder. Matthew knew there was no sense in looking for him.

In the late afternoon, as Matthew had just finished making some jerky, he had the feeling of being watched. He had a pretty good idea who was watching him. Slowly Matthew turned around. It was Thunder, looking and at him with the eye of a beggar. Matthew smiled, and then threw him a piece of jerky.

"There you go, Thunder."

That night he tied Thunder to a tree.

"See you in the morning, Thunder."

The next morning Thunder was gone. He had chewed through the rope.

Carlos returned from one of the other camps mid-morning. Not seeing the wolf, he asked, "Where's Thunder?"

Matthew told him what had happened in the last two days.

"You must let him go. Let him be free. Thunder was born free so let him live free. At night we've heard howling. The howls coming from the mountains are of his own kind calling Thunder back to the wild where he belongs. If Thunder wants to come back to us he can, but only when he wants to. You must accept what's best for Thunder. You have your freedom, now let him have his. Even though you saved him, Thunder doesn't belong to you. He belongs to the wilderness. Thunder should be free to live his life in Mother Nature's world, not the way you want him to live."

"You're right. It's just hard for me to let him go, but I know it's the right thing to do."

"After all, you still have me," Carlos said with a grin. Matthew looked at Carlos and they both laughed.

Once in a while, just like Carlos said, Thunder came back to visit. He would stay most of the day, then leave before dark. At times, he and Matthew would meet up in the mountains and hike the day together. Knowing Thunder was okay and always around, was good enough for Matthew.

It was that time of year again. Routinely, Carlos would be going down to Mexico. Carlos asked Matthew if he would be going with him.

"I think I'll stay here again for the winter. Tell everyone, especially Grandma, I said hello. I'll come down with you later in the year. Being with family during the holidays, I think, is great for you — but for me, holidays never really meant much. When we first met, I told you how I was shuffled from foster home to foster home.

"When the holidays came, even though I was supposed to be 'part of their family,' I never did fit in. They weren't my family. I never had a family and I knew for sure, I wasn't a part of their family. I would pretend I was enjoying their family holiday, but when I could, I would make up any excuse to go to my room or outside. I just wanted to be alone. Don't misunderstand me, Carlos. When it comes to you and your family, it's different. With your family, I have the feeling of belonging. I am very grateful Carlos, It's just me; I like being alone. I hope you understand."

"I do. It's just the way you grew up. Maybe nothing will ever change you. It's just who you are."

Carlos had been gone for over a month. Matthew was holed up in one of the camps. It had been snowing for two days, but had finally stopped. For Matthew, his routine was just like last winter: move between camps, hunt for fresh meat, and make items to trade at the end of winter. But most important of all, was staying warm.

Matthew was making an arrow when he heard a bark from outside. That could only mean one thing—Thunder. Matthew stepped outside of the cave and there he was, standing about twenty feet away.

"I'm glad to see you. Are you hungry?"

Thunder answered with two barks.

"Come in and I'll give you some jerky." They spent the rest of the day together. Then Thunder left. Off and on throughout the winter, Thunder would find Matthew no matter where he was.

CARLOS RETURNS FROM MEXICO

Matthew was waiting in the camp where he and Carlos were to meet. Carlos had never arrived this late. Matthew waited another week before he decided to go down to Mexico to find Carlos. Matthew wondered if he might have become sick, hurt, or worse yet, apprehended in Mexico. He wasn't going to wait any longer; he'd leave the next morning. While making himself ready for the journey, Matthew every once in a while, looked to see if Carlos was coming.

Later in the day Matthew was eating some deer stew. This time when he looked up, he saw Carlos coming into camp. As he came closer, Matthew could tell that he was all right. But there was something different about him.

Before Matthew could say anything, Carlos grabbed him, hugged him, and spun the two of them around.

"What's wrong with you?" Matthew asked.

Carlos stopped, smiled, and started laughing. Then he yelled, "I'm a free man! I'm a free man!"

"Let me tell you what happened. Remember I told you that there were still two others left after the raid who worked for the drug cartel. My task force continued their investigation until they had enough evidence to prosecute one of them. When they interrogated him, he told them he would tell everything if they would go easy on him. He told them all about the three of them and their involvement with the drug cartel.

"They asked him about the night of the raid when I killed one of them. He told them that they knew that I was investigating them and that they were trying to kill me. He also told them that I had no connection with the drug cartel. I was completely innocent. After the investigation, all charges against me were dropped. It's all over the news in Mexico and the United States.

"I stayed in Mexico and walked the streets of my town with my family and spent time with friends. You don't know what it feels like to be free, Matthew. I can come and go as I please. I don't have to hide anymore. I can start my life over again from where I left off. I've also been reinstated in the task force."

"I'm so happy and excited for you that I feel like it's me that's free."

"Everyone wanted to have a big fiesta and celebrate. I told them not until I came and got you, my brother."

Three days later, they left for Mexico. Before Carlos started his hike out of the mountains, he looked around one last time. It was hard for him to believe that he would never again have to live in hiding.

As they continued to descend the mountain, Carlos had the feeling that they were being followed. "It's probably just my imagination, I'm just being overly cautious," he thought to himself.

"When we get down below to where there's a hiking trail, I can't wait to see someone and say hello," said Carlos.

They were still high in the mountains following one of the game trails atop an arroyo. Matthew was leading the way and Carlos followed, whistling and singing. Matthew smiled to himself. He was glad that Carlos was finally free. The game trail went though a large formation of boulders.

"When we get to the clearing past the boulders, let's take a break," said Matthew.

"Good idea," replied Carlos.

They went around the last boulder with Matthew still leading the way. When they reached the clearing, they were both taken by surprise. Waiting for them was the one-eyed black bear standing on his hind legs, growling and moving his head back and forth in anger. The bear lowered himself to the ground and charged.

Before Matthew could do anything, Carlos grabbed him and pushed him into the arroyo. Knowing that Matthew was safe, Carlos turned to face the huge, lunging bear. But before Carlos could do anything, the bear violently knocked him to the ground. Carlos was able to pull his knife before the bear was on top of him. He stabbed the bear a few times, but to no avail. The bear was just too fast and powerful. He kept growling, clawing, and biting Carlos, tearing and ripping at his body.

Finally, the bear stopped. Carlos lay motionless. The bear stood over Carlos' body waiting for the slightest movement. There was none. The black bear knew then that finally, he had evened the score with his old enemy.

When Matthew opened his eyes, the first thing he felt was the caked blood and matted hair on the side of his head. There was a deep long gash, but the bleeding had stopped. He didn't know how long he had been unconscious at the bottom of the arroyo. It took him a few minutes to piece together what had happened. He remembered Carlos had pushed him out of the way of the bear. He must climb out of the arroyo and find Carlos. Spells of dizziness slowed his climb. When he reached the top, he almost went into a state of shock.

Carlos was a bloody mess. Claw marks, torn clothes, and shredded meat in some places was all that was left. Matthew had seen blood and bodies in Afghanistan, but it never affected him like this. The bear was nowhere in sight.

He fell to his knees and began throwing up. He continued gagging even when there was nothing left. A feeling that he never had before was slowly taking over his body. This feeling brought on tears that had been harbored most of his adult life. Now the tears flowed freely, almost nonstop. He didn't know, how long he cried. Finally, he could cry no more.

Being a loner all of his life made him emotionally stronger than most men. But knowing what he had to do would take all of his strength to bring him back to his senses.

Slowly, he got to his feet and walked over to where Carlos' lifeless body lay. Matthew picked up what was left of his friend. Very slowly he began his trip to the top of the mountain to bury Carlos. It took two days to reach the top, but seemed like forever.

"This is the most beautiful place in the mountains," he remembered Carlos saying.

Matthew said out loud, "You're right Carlos. This is the most beautiful place in the wilderness."

Digging with his bare hands and a branch, he dug a hole as deep as he could before reaching solid rock. He wrapped Carlos in a blanket and placed him in the grave. He covered Carlos with pine boughs and then dirt. Matthew gathered rocks and began placing them on the grave, stacking them nice and high. A slight smile appeared when he remembered what Carlos said, "Don't let the predators dig me up. I don't want to be part of Mother Nature's food chain."

He also remembered when they laughed together. Matthew finished with a prayer that Carlos had taught him.

Still on his knees, once again he became sick to his stomach, and again started crying like an infant.

Throughout his entire life, he had prided and protected himself with his invisible shield, but he had no protection against anything like this.

Carlos was his mentor and his best friend. He was the only real friend Matthew had ever known. They both knew that there would come a time when they would separate; Carlos would return to Mexico and Matthew would live in the mountains. Neither ever thought death would be the reason for their separation.

Matthew built a fire and stayed near Carlos' grave for two days and nights. On the third morning, he started to hike down the mountain. With the grave still in sight, he turned around and said aloud, "I will never forget you, Carlos. Thanks for being my friend."

He has no particular place to go. He is glad that the camps have plenty of food and other supplies because he doesn't feel like hunting, or doing anything else. He still can't believe that he will never see Carlos again. He can't stop remembering how Carlos had pushed him out of the way of that bear. He had saved his life; Carlos knew that it was he the bear was after.

When Matthew arrived at one of the camps, Thunder was there. Thunder came over and put his head on Matthew's lap and started whining.

"You know, don't you boy? You miss him too."

Matthew didn't feel much like eating. Later he finally cooked his dinner and ate a little. Matthew had trouble sleeping that night; he had the feeling something wasn't right.

Burial is supposed to be the closure of death, but for Matthew, burying Carlos wasn't the last thing he had to do. He lay awake for hours. Finally, it came to him. He knew what had to be done and how he'd do it. He couldn't wait until morning.

MATTHEW'S REVENGE

The next morning Matthew was up earlier than usual. Thunder could sense that something was going on.

"Thunder, how would you like to help me kill that bear?" Thunder barked and growled. He ran two feet in front of Matthew, then turned around and ran back.

"Good boy."

They hiked to the cache. Matthew took the copper-tipped arrows and returned to camp. The arrows were no good. Matthew began by making new shafts and trimming new feathers for each arrow. He sharpened the arrowheads to a razor-sharp edge; the edges from the base to the tip of the arrowheads were serrated.

Two days later, everything he needed was ready. In honor of Carlos, Matthew decided to use Carlos' bow. He filled his quiver with arrows.

With his revenge planned, Matthew retired early. He woke up right before daylight.

With Thunder by his side, they made their way toward the mountain range and into the arroyo to the bear's cave.

It wasn't hard to locate. Bear tracks were very distinct on the trail. There was only one trail in and out of the arroyo. At the end of the arroyo, Matthew saw the cave behind the open area in front of him. He climbed out of the arroyo. From atop the arroyo, Matthew was able to look down into the cave. He moved closer to within range of the bow. He couldn't afford to miss. Once in position, Matthew had no way of knowing if the bear was even in the cave. But he knew how to find out.

Matthew whispered, "Thunder, go down and find out if the bear is in the cave. If he is, get him to come out. Be careful, I don't want anything to happen to you. Understand, boy?"

Thunder barked and ran down toward the cave. Once in front, he began barking and growling. He ran close to the entrance, and then retreated in a circular movement. The wolf repeated this several times. Matthew heard the bear let out a growl from inside his cave. Thunder retreated even farther.

Matthew watched the cave's entrance, waiting for the bear to come out. Finally, he came out of his cave.

Thunder backed up farther, barking and growling. The bear was becoming angry. He began growling and pawing the ground. Now Thunder ran toward the bear, but stopped before barking and retreating; this was his way of challenging the bear.

The bear had finally had enough. He stood up on his hind legs, growling in anger. If he went back down on all fours, Matthew knew it would charge Thunder and attack him.

Matthew had a clear shot. He knew he would have to be fast and shoot as many arrows into that bear as he possibly could. He released arrow after arrow into the bear's heart.

The bear was now howling and screaming in pain. He dropped down on all fours and tried to lunge forward, but couldn't. Matthew shot two more arrows into its neck. The bear was still moving, but had collapsed to the ground to slowly die.

Matthew knew the bear would be dead before too long. He came down from the top of the arroyo. Now he stood directly in front of the bear. Matthew knew that if the bear could kill him, he would. The bear's only eye was open and its head was barely moving. Now it was no threat to anyone.

Matthew took another arrow out of his quiver. He looked at the bear and let the last arrow fly.

"This one's for Carlos."

The arrow found its mark, right through the good eye and into the brain.

Matthew heard a wheezing sound as the last breath of air left the bear's body. He walked away with Thunder by his side. Matthew turned around for one last look at the dead bear.

"Mother Nature can finish you," he said. Avenging the death of his friend gave Matthew some feeling of satisfaction, but it wasn't enough to overcome the sick, empty feeling still inside him. "How long will it take for it to go away?" Matthew wondered out loud.

They returned to camp. When Matthew awoke the next morning Thunder was gone. Matthew stayed in camp two more days. He knew he must tell Carlos' family what had happened. This was the most difficult thing he'd ever had to do. He stayed another three days. "No sense in waiting any longer," he told himself.

Matthew left for Mexico. Stopping at the two ranches on the way, he told the cousins about Carlos. By the time he arrived at Carlos' house, the family knew. Having a difficult time emotionally, he told them everything that had happened. After only staying two days, he decided to leave. He said good-bye to everyone and started his return journey. On his way back a sad thought entered his mind. "This was my first trip to Mexico without Carlos."

When he was back in New Mexico, he hiked higher into the mountains. He never even stopped to see Bill like he routinely did. Matthew didn't care to be around anybody.

Six months had passed since Carlos' death. Matthew's memory wouldn't let him forget that day. He remembered how Carlos pushed him out of the way of the bear and saved his life. He knew he had to stop thinking about it. But how? Sometimes when in camp, Matthew would look up expecting to see Carlos.

Matthew stayed high in the mountains for the next three months. He knew and understood life in the mountains. He could survive in any situation. Matthew knew and understood the signs of Mother Nature; He knew when the changes in the weather would occur. He knew about the habits of the different kinds of animals, and could read their signs as well as track and find them. All this Matthew knew and understood. When Matthew thought about himself, he was confused; he had no understanding of himself.

One day as he was hiking, he was surprised to see Thunder come running toward him. The wolf jumped on Matthew, knocking him to the ground. They wrestled around for a while.

"I'm sure glad to see you," said Matthew. They went back to camp. They stayed together for two days. While hiking on the third day, Thunder left. Matthew watched as Thunder disappeared.

Being reunited with Thunder was uplifting for him. "I needed that," he said to himself. He continued hiking to a campsite for the night. He couldn't stop thinking of Carlos again. This time, however, his thoughts were different. For some reason, he remembered Carlos telling him about Grandma. When the family had problems, they would go to his grandma seeking her advice. "Why did I think about that? I wonder if she could help me?" he asked himself.

Matthew changed his mind about where he would camp for the night. Instead, he began hiking his way out of the mountains, going to south to Mexico.

It's been almost a year since Bill had seen Matthew. Bill was worried. One morning he was dusting shelves and restocking supplies, when he heard the bell at the door jingle. He looked toward the door, hoping it was Matthew. It wasn't.

A couple had just entered.

"Can I help you?"

"We would like some information," the woman said.

"What kind of information?"

"We're staying at one of the campgrounds. At night everyone sits around the campfire socializing. Stories are told. More than one story tells of a man that is sometimes seen with a wolf. The man and wolf have come to the rescue of campers and hikers in distress. We want to know if they are just stories. The camp manager said that you might know of this man."

"Yes, I do," Bill replied. "He never really told me too much of what he does in the wilderness. Some of the people he's saved have stopped by here and have told me about their experiences. Yes, the stories you have heard are real. Matter of fact, I was thinking of him this morning. He hasn't been in to trade in a long time. That isn't like him."

"Aren't you worried?" the woman asked.

"Yes, I am. I don't like to think about it. There's an old saying around here, 'If you live long enough in the mountains, you die in the mountains.'

"Have you gone out looking for him?" the man asked.

"No, at my age I have no business out in the wilderness."

"Have you sent out a search party?" the woman asked.

"No. Sending out a search party would do no good. I'll guarantee you that if he's still alive, they would never find him. Men like him don't want to be found."

"How can anyone live alone, especially in the mountains?" the man asked.

"It takes a different kind of person. Some people like being alone. Matthew has been alone all his life. He knows how to survive. Survival is more mental, than physical. He once told me the secret of living alone is having a 'satisfied mind'. Actually, Matthew isn't alone," Bill said with a smile. "He has his wolf, Thunder. He also spends some time with another mountain man."

Bill and the couple talked for another hour before they left.

After they were gone, Bill walked over to his chair and sat down. Midnight jumped up onto his lap. As Bill pet him, he said, "I hope Matthew's all right."

GRANDMA TALKS TO MATTHEW

Matthew arrived at Carlos' house late in the afternoon. The children were outside playing. When they saw Matthew, they ran into the house yelling, "Matthew's here! Matthew's here!"

Their mother met him at the door. She smiled and gave him a big hug. "We're glad to see you," she said. One of Carlos' brothers was also there visiting. He too was glad to see Matthew.

A big dinner was planned to celebrate Matthew's arrival. After dinner everyone sat around talking for hours. When the brother had left, everyone went to bed.

Matthew was the first to awake in the morning. He walked into the kitchen and made himself coffee, remembering that he and Carlos were the only ones that drank coffee.

After everyone else had awakened and eaten breakfast, the kids left for school. Carlos's wife had to do errands. After she had left, Matthew decided that this would be a good time to talk to Grandma. He walked down the hallway towards Grandma's room. Her door was closed. Lightly, he knocked on the door.

"Grandma, are you awake?"

Grandma told him to come in and sit down.

"I have to talk to you about Carlos."

"I've been waiting for you; I could tell when I saw you yesterday, that you were troubled."

"You know?"

"Yes," answered Grandma.

"It's still hard for me to accept his death. I can't believe he's gone. I don't mind being alone, but he's always on my mind. Also, the dreams of my mother are coming back more and more," Matthew said.

"First, let's talk about your mother and why you still have dreams of her. Maybe I can help you understand why she left you. You were a little boy when she left you at the orphanage. You were too young to understand why she never returned. It wasn't because she didn't love you. I know, as every mother knows, that a mother's love is never-ending.

"I want to tell you a story about a poor Chiricahua couple and their three-year old son. They lived in a shack outside a small village in Mexico. To find work to support his family, the husband walked from village to village, sometimes for days and even weeks. One time, he was gone longer than usual. The wife knew that something had happened to him; she waited for weeks, then months. He never returned.

"Left alone to provide for her son, she did the best she could. But before too long, she and her son ended up in the village, living in the streets. Feeling ashamed, she begged for food and shelter.

"During the first winter, she became terribly ill. There was no doctor in the village. One of the men offered to take her in his wagon to a doctor in one of the other villages. She hated to leave her son, but had no choice. His mother told him how much she loved him and promised him that as soon as she was well, she would return.

"He was left with a couple that had a little girl her son's age. She felt that her son would be well-taken care of.

"Because of the seriousness of her illness, the mother was gone longer than she wanted to be. She never stopped thinking of her son, and how happy and excited he would be when she returned. These thoughts helped her during her time of healing.

"Finally, she was completely healed. On the way back to the village, all she thought about was that they would be together again. When the mother arrived at the village, she went directly to the house where she had left her son. It was burned and in rubble.

"She was told that while she was gone, a fire had swept through the village destroying five houses. She asked about the family and her son. They were all right, she was told. The family had moved to another village. The mother went to that village, only to find out that they had moved again. No one knew where.

"In the years that followed, she went from village to village searching for her son. Eventually, the mother remarried. She had three more children, and was happy again. She never forgot her son and prayed that she would someday find him.

"I told you that story because, just like your mother, what happened in the story was not the mother's choice. In life, things happen that we have no control over.

"As you grew older, did you ever ask yourself why your mother did what she did? Was she sick? Was she dying? Could she not afford to take care of you anymore? Why didn't she come back? Matthew, it wasn't all about you.

"You told me that every night you cried yourself to sleep. How many nights do you think your mother cried? You will never know how much pain and suffering she went through.

"You also told me that you hated her. It's normal for young children to use the word "hate." It's used when we're angry with someone, or when we don't understand what's happened. It's a word we've heard, but do we really know what it means at a young age?

"Hate is a feeling of weakness. It's made up of anger, hurt, and sadness. Love is a much stronger feeling, a feeling of happiness, joy, understanding, and forgiveness. Yes, there is also hurt. Unlike hate, love is much stronger, and in time, can overcome hurt.

"At first you were angry with your mother, and then you hated her so much that, as the years passed and she never returned, you told yourself she was dead. That was the only way you could get back at her.

"Your mother loved you so much that she did what she had to do. It was her love that she gave and left with you that made you strong, not your hate for her. Her love was so strong that, if something would happen and you were never together again, she knew you could go on without her. The reason you haven't been able to stop dreaming about and remembering her, Matthew, is because what you've felt for her all this time is love, not hate.

"To protect yourself from being hurt again, you built a wall around yourself. You've survived all this time by standing alone. You've avoided any emotional relationships. You've stayed a safe distance from everybody and even life itself. You haven't lived Matthew, you've only existed.

"Before you saved Carlos, you were like a lone rock in the middle of the desert. All around that rock there is life, consisting of birds, animals, and plants. Together, everything makes up life in the desert. Plants and animals need each other to ensure their survival. The rock stands alone from its surroundings.

"What does a rock have to offer? It's just a rock. Life goes on all around it. With the passing of time, changes occur that the rock has no control over. Eventually, that rock will begin to deteriorate. Little by little, it will start to crumble until it turns to sand, and then becomes part of life in the desert.

"Fate brought you and Carlos together. All the time that you spent together or apart, the bond became stronger and stronger. At the same time, that wall you built around yourself for protection became weaker and weaker. You had no idea what was happening. Carlos taught you everything he knew. He gave of himself, but you didn't realize that in return, you gave him your friendship; something that you told yourself you would never let happen with anyone. Like the rock, you had no control of what was happening.

"He taught you how to survive in the wild. He was not only your mentor, but your best friend. After Carlos was killed, the wall that you built to protect yourself crumbled. When it did, your protection was gone. You finally became part of life. But now, you are confused and lost. Unlike the rock, people are made of emotions. You don't know how to cope with your feelings. Once again you felt abandoned, just like when your mother left you.

"It was not Carlos' death, but your love for him that has left you with that empty feeling. Don't remember him by his dying, but by his living. Remember the good times you two spent together. If sometimes you feel like talking to Carlos, go ahead and talk. That's one of the ways that some people cope with death. It's part of the healing process. It's only normal.

"Everyone deals with death in different ways, and have different time tables for accepting death. But remember Matthew, if too much time goes by and you can't accept Carlos' death, it's possible that you're only feeling sorry for yourself.

"Put your memories in your heart, Matthew. When you think of him, the warmth you feel inside will bring a smile to your face, and maybe even a chuckle, or a little laughter. It's only normal that you'll feel sad at times, but the majority of your memories will be   happy ones.

"Listen to your heart, Matthew. Feel what it tells you. Follow your heart and it will lead you to peace of mind.

"Carlos' family has put his death behind them, and moved on with their lives, but he's in their hearts. They will never forget him. That's what you need to do, Matthew. Put him in your heart and he will always be with you."

Matthew looked at Grandma. His eyes began to water.

"Carlos taught me everything I know about the wild. Whenever I needed him, he was always there. I really depended on him. Even when we were separated, I worried about him."

"You've told me how you needed and depended on him. Did you ever think that Carlos needed you too?"

"What do you mean?" Matthew asked.

"There's something about Carlos that you need to know. My family has always known that Carlos was more Apache than Mexican. That was the reason that he had the strong desire to learn about and live the Apache way. He could live anywhere and survive.

"His other strong trait was his natural ability to help people and interact with them. That's one reason he joined the police force. He also liked the comradeship. But above everything else, his family came first. He loved his family.

"There's a reason why I'm telling you this Matthew. Remember when you found him almost drowned in the river?"

"Sure," answered Matthew.

"After that happened, one of the times when he came to see us, he told me that the solitude had become too much for him. Hiding and living in fear became more than he was capable of handling. He could not stand being away from his family.

"He never slept the night before he tried to cross the river. He lay awake thinking of his future. It looked hopeless. How much longer would he have to live in the wilderness? How many more months or years before he would be free to rejoin his family? Each secret visit became more and more difficult for everyone; leaving was especially hard for him. The more he thought about everything, the more he felt he didn't have a choice. Carlos decided not to put himself or his family through that traumatic experience anymore. He might never be free, but he could set them free to live a normal life.

"Because of the melting snow, the river was higher and swifter than normal. Carlos had crossed that river many times before. He knew that now was not the time to cross. He took a careless chance. Carlos told me that he didn't care anymore. If his body was ever found, no one would ever know what had happened; they would only think that it was an accident.

"As he entered the river, the current was so swift that his legs were swept out from under him. Carlos fell into the raging river and was barely able to keep his head above water. As he started going under, his life flashed before him. He saw his wife, kids, and entire family, but not himself. That's when he realized that he wanted to live. Carlos began fighting the current. He was trying to swim to shore. The strong under-current kept pulling him down, deeper and deeper. He was no match for the water's force. Carlos started swallowing water.

"He was slammed into a large rock. The roaring sound of the river became silent. Everything turned dark. That's the last thing he remembered.

"When Carlos awoke the morning after you saved him, he couldn't believe he was still alive. Carlos sat by the fire looking at you. That's when Carlos realized that fate had brought you two together. Everything happens for a reason. He didn't know why, but he was glad to be alive.

"He never told you, but you became his pillar of strength. You had given him new hope and a reason to live. Carlos' feeling of loneliness and isolation disappeared. His visits became easier. What he enjoyed most was teaching you all he knew about survival. He knew that this was something you really wanted and needed. Carlos also felt that teaching you survival skills, in a very small way, was his gift to you for saving his life. More importantly to him, you became his only friend in the wilderness.

"Carlos was saved because it was not time for him to leave us. He was given more time so he would be alive when the criminal charges against him were dropped. This also removed the black cloud that would always be with his family the rest of their lives. My grandson died a free man. That's the real reason for you saving him. This is something that I thought you needed to know.

"Remember everything we talked about today. Look at your past, your present, and your future. Like I told you before, follow your heart and it will lead you in the right direction."

"Grandma, thank you for everything," said Matthew. Before he walked through the door, he stopped and asked.

"Did the Apache woman ever find her son?"

"No," answered Grandma. "Remember, I told you that your mother never forgot you. Like her, I never forgot my son. Mothers will always love their children."

Matthew walked out of the house into the street. He walked until he was in front of the orphanage. There he saw the children playing in the yard. When one little girl saw him, she waved. Matthew smiled and waved back.

"I think I'll spend some time at the orphanage before I go back to the wilderness," he said to himself. He stayed two more weeks with Carlos' family, and helped at the orphanage.

MATTHEW RETURNS TO THE POST

Matthew began his trip back to New Mexico. During the hike back all he could think about were his talks with Grandma.

When he was back in New Mexico, he headed straight for the high mountains. Because of nice weather, there would be more hikers and campers in the wilderness.

He hiked high into the mountains where he knew there were no trails or hikers. He moved from camp to camp with no particular destination in mind. He couldn't stop thinking of what Grandma told him about his mother, Carlos, and himself— mainly himself.

"Follow you heart and it will lead you to peace of mind," he kept hearing her say.

One night before he went to sleep, the dream of his mother came back. For the first time in his life he had a different feeling about her. He thought about how hard everything must have been for her. Then surprisingly, he asked himself, "I wonder where she is now?"

The next morning he awoke and decided to hike to the most beautiful place in the wilderness. He didn't understand why, but he wanted to visit Carlos' grave. He hiked to the top. Reluctantly, but still wanting to, he walked into the opening and sat down.

Leaning back against a large rock, he looked around. "It's so peaceful and quiet," he said to himself. "Nothing else is here except white clouds, blue sky, and of course, Carlos."

He looked over at the grave. His first feeling was that of sadness. He started remembering the things that they did together. The more he thought about everything, the more he experienced a warm feeling inside. It was a different feeling, a special feeling of friendship that he knew he would never forget.

Before too long, Matthew was asleep. He didn't know how long he had slept. It was starting to get dark and a little on the chilly side when he awoke.

"I'll build us a fire, Carlos." He was taken back by what he just said. He smiled, feeling good inside. "I'm talking to you, just like Grandma said I might do."

He continued to talk to Carlos. "I remembered what you told me about Grandma. You were right. Talking to her has really helped me."

"There's one thing I want to do for you, Carlos. When your son is old enough to make the trip from Mexico, I want to bring him here to visit you."

"I'm going to stay here for a few days. I need to go down to the Post to see Bill. He probably thinks something's happened to me. It's been over a year since he's seen me.

"By the way, there's something I think you need to know. Thunder and I took care of that one-eyed bear. He won't kill anyone else."

Matthew stayed two more days before saying good-bye to Carlos. "I'll be back," he said. Feeling good about himself, he began hiking down the mountain.

Bill was sitting on the front porch of the trading post. It

had become his every-day routine lately. He told himself he was waiting for customers, but he knew the real reason: Bill was hoping to see Matthew come hiking in from the mountains. It had been too long since he'd seen Matthew. Bill couldn't stop worrying. He didn't want to believe it, but he had a terrible feeling that Matthew was dead.

Bill got out of his chair and started to walk back inside. A car pulled up. Bill turned around. A man on crutches got out of the car and hobbled toward him.

Bill saw that the man also had cuts on his face and arms. It seemed to Bill like he had been in some kind of accident.

As the man stepped up on the porch he asked, "Mind if I sit down? Hobbling around on these crutches can wear one out."

"Sure, sit down," answered Bill.

"I'm going to buy some snacks, then head home," said the man. "I've been longer in these mountains than I had planned. I should've left here two weeks ago. I've been laid up at the second camp up the hill from here, recovering from my accident. I had a bad fall."

"What happened?"

"Every so often you hear on the news about someone lost in the wilderness, or maybe injured while out hiking. I know what I'm doing when it comes to hiking and camping. I never thought that anything like I've seen on the news would ever happen to me.

"I drove down from Albuquerque to spend three or four days hiking. The second day I was on one of the lower trails. I always try to hike on established trails for safety. According to the marker along the lower trail, the trail I was on would connect to a higher trail eventually. I decided to hike straight up from the lower trail—a short cut. It didn't appear to be dangerous. I was almost to the top. I could see the upper trail. I slipped on the loose gravel and down I went. Before I could do anything to stop my fall, I was tumbling head over heels for what seemed like forever. I stopped falling when I landed on the bottom trail. I knew I was hurt, but I didn't know how bad. My head was cut and my vision was blurry. My shirt and pants were torn. My arms and legs were cut and bleeding; my right ankle and leg were beginning to swell. I tried to stand up, but the pain was too much. I became dizzy, so I sat back down.

"I could only hope that another hiker would come by. My backpack, which contained my cell phone, was somewhere on the side of the mountain. I didn't know where. There was nothing I could do, but sit and wait for some kind of help. I didn't know how much time had passed. It would soon be dark. If I didn't get help I would really be in trouble.

"Then I heard it. The sound ran shivers up my spine; it was the growl of a wolf. There he was coming out of the brush. Looking directly at me, he kept growling. Where there's one, there are more. I knew that they run around in packs, numbering from four to as many as eight in numbers.

"I carry a 9mm pistol, but along with everything else, it was in my backpack. I knew I was dead. Not that it would have done any good, but slowly I grabbed the nearest stick. I gathered some rocks that were close to me. I could throw them at the wolf. I kept looking at the wolf and he kept staring back at me. I was scared and shaking, waiting for his attack. I was ready to defend myself. I didn't see the other wolves, but I knew they were out there, also ready to attack.

"The only thing I could hope for was that when the pack

attacked, it would be over quick. I closed my eyes and said a quick prayer. When I opened them, standing next to the wolf, I saw what looked like a mountain man. The first words out of my mouth were, 'Thank you, Lord!'

"I remember hearing the man call the wolf by name. He called him Thunder. I guess the pain and the trauma was too much. Everything became blurry and then I passed out. I awoke to voices. There were three other hikers around me. One of them said they would carry me out. I told them my backpack was somewhere on the side of the mountain.

"'No it isn't. It's here next to you,' one of the hikers said.

"I looked down at my side, and there it was. The mountain man must have brought it down.'"

Bill was excited. "When did this happen?"

"Two and a half weeks ago, give or take a few days."

"Did the man tell you his name?"

"No. Besides that, I was in so much pain when he found me, I didn't ask. He didn't talk much. I do know he called the wolf Thunder. I'll never forget that wolf glaring at me."

Bill didn't want to get too excited. It could be Matthew or the other mountain man with Matthew. Thunder could have been with either one of them.

"What did the mountain man look like?"

"I really don't remember that much about him. I just know he looked like a man that lived in the mountains. You have to remember I was scared, hurt, and not seeing too clearly. I've told you what happened, and all I remembered."

"I hope you didn't mind my questions," Bill said. "There's a man I know who lives in the mountains. I just wondered if it might have been him. He does have a wolf."

"Really? Sorry I couldn't have been more help to you," replied the man.

"That's all right. It could have been worse."

"Sure could've," said the man. "If it wasn't for that mountain man, I would have died up there." The man bought what he needed, then left.

Bill walked back into the store. "I wonder if it was Matthew," he asked himself. He sat down in his chair. It was his nap time.

Three days later, Bill and Midnight were in the back room. Bill looked at Midnight and asked, "Is that all you can do? Just sit there and watch me?"

Bill heard the jingle of the door bell. "We have a customer," he said to Midnight.

"Go see who it is."

Midnight didn't move. Bill walked out of the back room and into the store. He looked towards the door. To his surprise and relief, there was Matthew. Bill couldn't believe it. The first words out of his mouth were, "I thought you were dead." Matthew smiled, and then laughed.

"Sorry I was gone so long. I had my reasons. Let me tell you what happened."

Bill said, "I hope you have a good excuse."

Matthew walked over to the bulletin board. Pointing to the picture of Carlos, Matthew said. "He was my friend in the wilderness. I'm sorry I couldn't tell you before, but that was who I was with. He was a fugitive, not a mountain man."

Matthew told Bill all about Carlos and Mexico. When he had finished, Bill just stood there speechless. "All this time I've been trading with a fugitive."

"You can take down the wanted poster now," said Matthew.

They talked for hours. In the afternoon it was time for Matthew to leave. "What are you going to do now with your friend gone?"

"Go back into the mountains where I belong. Thunder and I will be just fine. A few times a year I'll go to Mexico to see Carlos' family. I've also started working at the orphanage. It's helping me to understand more about myself."

Before he left, Bill said, "Matthew, seeing you again has made this old man mighty happy."

"I promise I won't stay gone as long," Matthew said with a smile. He picked up his supplies, said good-bye, and walked out the door.

Bill watched as Matthew headed back into the mountains. In no time at all, he was out of sight.

Bill knew that Matthew's search for a place to belong had finally ended. More importantly, he knew that Matthew had finally found himself and peace of mind. By the end of the day, Bill was tired, but he didn't mind that at all.

It had been one of his best days in a long time. Because now Bill also had peace of mind; He knew that Matthew was alive and doing well. Bill lay down on his bed. "It wouldn't take me but a minute to fall asleep," he said to himself. As he was just starting to doze, he heard Midnight meowing at the back door.

"Uh-oh," said Bill out loud, "I forgot to put that darn cat out."

ABOUT THE AUTHOR

Randy McCowan and his wife Sally moved to Deming in 1995 from Escondido, California. After living in Deming for two years, he built his own ghost town, something he always wanted to do. The ghost town is called Olmesquite.

McCowan is involved in Old West research and considered one of the area's best historians. While writing his first book, "El Perdido, The Lost One," he traveled over 2,500 miles through Arizona and New Mexico, talking to dozens of Apaches on several reservations.

His second book, "The Guardian in the Wilderness" is the story of a young man learning to survive in the wilderness. Not only is it a story of his survival in the wilderness, but a story of his surviving life itself.

When not writing or working in his ghost town, Randy is hiking the mountains and deserts of New Mexico. He believes that telling stories of the Old West keeps history alive.

Guardian in the Wilderness